The Fifth Floor

This is a work of fiction. Names, characters, places, and incidents either are the product of the author's imagination or are used fictitiously, and any resemblance to actual persons living or dead, business establishments, events, or locales is entirely coincidental.

THE FIFTH FLOOR

Cool Gus Publishing
coolgus.com

Cool Gus Publishing
http://coolgus.com

ISBN: 9781621252993

The Fifth Floor

BOB MAYER

*Consciousness is a much smaller part of our mental life than we are
conscious of, because we cannot be conscious of what we are not
conscious of.*
Julian Jaynes: **The Origin of Consciousness in the Breakdown of the
Bicameral Mind**.

Lara's Journal

BEFORE THERE WAS JUST ME NOW, there was a bunch of other stuff that I don't remember. People keep telling me I should remember, but maybe if you can't remember there's a reason.

I know a few things: I'm supposed to be sixteen; I have short, sorta mousy brown hair, which should be brushed more than it does, and nice legs. I like my toes; they are long and very straight. My boobs are smaller than Dr. Jenkins but bigger than that total flat-chested bitch night nurse, Mary-Louise,. Really, is that even a name? Parents couldn't have picked just one? I guess I shouldn't say that cause I don't really know my name. Dr. Jenkins tells me that it's Lily Cole because she does have that school ID that says that's my name and that I'm sixteen. But I've stared at that picture a few times and it's not me. I don't know much, but I know that's not me. Maybe if all my hair were much longer and brushed out like that it could be me. But, then it would still be someone who could be me but isn't me.

I'm not sure who I am, but I'm pretty fucking sure that I'm not Lily Cole, with all that name entails.

I don't feel like a Lily. Parents don't stare at a baby that is not Lily and say--oh, my, let's call her Lily. So, I'm not her. I can understand why everyone here thinks I am. They have that stupid ID card. It's from a George Washington High School. Seriously? Why not Abraham Lincoln High? How generic can you get?

I just let it pass. I have this weird idea that I'm a person who let's stuff float on by. Doesn't fight it cause really is there a point to that? You think I can change anyone's mind here who thinks I'm Lily when I'm not actually Lily? Or that I'm not sixteen? I think I'm older, which is sorta a bitch 'cause when you remember nothing it'd be nice if you were sixteen and sort of naïve and everything is ahead of you, but I'm not naive; at least not in a sixteen-year-old way. And there doesn't seem to be much ahead of me.

I got a hard bed, a dirty sink, and a toilet that smells like urine soaked used sports equipment all in one small, square room—isn't it actually a cell if it's locked from the outside? But they call it my room. There's a tiny mirror, I do stare into that, and I don't look sixteen, which is weird cause I

1

don't remember what sixteen should look like. That's the hardest part of all of this; I can't think much cause there isn't anything to think about because the memories aren't there but I still feel things. And I feel like I'm older but no one wants to hear that cause all they care about is that I accept that I'm the person in the wallet of some torn pair of jeans.

Really? Would you base all of what you know about yourself on a wallet in a pair of jeans, which frankly, I don't feel that I would have ever worn. They look like old granny jeans and I stare at my long legs and pretty toes and think no one with a pair of legs as nice as mine would be wearing those old baggy frumpy jeans intended to hid the imperfections.

The shirt is even worse. Some calico striped thing that no girl with my flat stomach and perky round tits would wear. Or not the girl I am now. Maybe the girl I was then, but if that's who I was, I got no real inclination to care about her. This girl in the mirror, Lara, because in my head my name is Lara, she'd be in skinny jeans to show off these legs, and a tank top to show off this stomach and boobs. Or, the part of me that is Lara is just gone and those are my clothes and Lily is my name and then I did kill my mother, my father, my little sister, and my even littler brother.

But, when you can't remember anything do you want that to be the thing you want find under some rock in your head?

I don't think so.

I'm writing this and will take it with me cause I do need some words to help keep what is real for me. Just in case I can't remember now, when its later, like I can't remember the past, now. I had to re-read that, and yeah, it makes sense. As much as anything. Which means not much at all.

What's real right now is that I wouldn't wear those jeans or that shirt and that my name isn't Lily.

Just cause I can't remember doesn't mean I'm her. Actually, I sorta think I'm not her because any girl who could wear that crap; she wouldn't forget a thing. Did I mention that shirt was ironed? Yeah, ironed creases in the sleeves. Yeah, even though it was covered in blood when they showed it to me, but I knew right away that I don't iron and if I don't iron, then who did? The mother they say I killed? Who would kill a mother who ironed their shirt for them?

And I don't feel like an orphan. I just don't and even if I killed them, there should be some part of me that at least feels the loss of them. But, I don't. I just don't. Sorry. And I know I would feel it; nNot like some of the others here who don't feel anything.

Or feel too much. Not sure which is worse.

I have family out there. Somewhere. I know it.

So, I'm leaving here tonight and taking these pages with me. I'll keep writing on them because only in these words is there a Lara and yeah—

I'm Lara in skinny blue jeans and a tank top with a mom and dad still out there. Or I'd miss them. And maybe a brother and sister. Because I'd really miss that brother and sister, but how can you miss people who never existed or still exist? I mean, even I can do that leap in what passes for my brain.

Really—I should just believe the people who tell me my name is Lily?
I don't think so.

Haifa, Israel

"Consciousness was upon him before he could get out of the way."
Kingsley Amis

STOREFRONT AWNINGS FLAPPED in the offshore breeze and the odor from open-air cooking by street vendors laced the air. Lunchtime was peak traffic for the seaside marketplace.

The smell of food made Lukas hungry, which was odd given his current circumstances, with a bomb strapped around his body.

He understood the timing, standing among all the people crowded tight, talking, laughing, eating, and unaware.

But he didn't understand the reason *why* he was here. He didn't remember where he came from before here, other than the darkness of the cellar where the bomb had been cinched to his body while someone whispered instructions in his ear.

He had no idea how he'd ended up in that cellar or what was before that.

Sweat trickled down his chest and along his spine. He was hot, although it was cool with the Mediterranean breeze. The outside coat was appropriate for the weather but not the vest underneath, with the layer of explosive and the pockets full of nails and ball bearings.

So why was *he* here?

Not far away, a baby cried. Lukas looked up at the sky. Clear blue, not a cloud. He looked down at all the people who were going to die. His own death didn't factor into it, a consequence that seemed to be for someone else, some other young man's destiny.

Young women glanced in his direction, eyeing him, because he was a handsome teenager, on the verge of manhood, gifted with exemplary genes. He had dark, curly hair, pale skin, a square jaw, and wide shoulders. There was much promise ahead, if he lived into it. But there were others wondering about him for a completely different reason, as he stood still, doing nothing, not walking, not eating, not with anyone else. A distant part of his brain echoed words from the briefing in the bleak cellar. The man who'd drummed into him what to do over and over; that he wasn't supposed to draw attention. That some of those looking wouldn't see a handsome boy, they would see potential danger, because his coat was too thick, even with his wide shoulders, and this was Israel and everyone had voices in their own heads whispering of danger, of suicide vests.

Why was he here? Which led to a further question: why couldn't he remember why he was here? Who he was?

He could remember the cellar, the man, and the instructions.

Who was he before that?

Who was he now?

His slipped his right hand into the coat pocket, fingers curled around the clacker.

I should have been an I.

A person. An individual.

I was never an I. I was always part of other.

That was why he was here. Because others wanted him to be here.

I am 'We'.

Lukas felt the richness of the lives around her. The happiness, the pain, the despair, the hope, the innocence of the bawling baby.

I am 'We'.

He saw two boys on the beach, kicking a soccer ball and everything went blank for a moment, then he saw one of them as a man, still kicking a ball, but in a stadium in front of tens of thousands cheering fans. Not far away was a pregnant woman, and Lukas saw her giving birth, family gathered round, tears of joy, the baby blossoming into a girl, into a woman, who would also give birth and there would be a long line into the future from this one person. Two men were arguing some arcane issue and he saw them later this same day, one going home to his welcoming family, the other to a small apartment, a bottle, the TV remote, and a revolver on the nightstand next to his bed, one bullet loaded, five chambers empty.

Lukas staggered, dizzied from all that swirled in his mind. He pushed his way to a table where two teenage girls were eating lunch and grabbed the spare chair. He sat down on the cheap plastic seat, ignoring their questioning looks. He 'saw' the explosion rippling out from him, tearing apart the people, the shrapnel slicing into flesh, the death, the maiming, and all those futures cut off.

So many lives branching out from this moment. So random, yet all that would cease with a twitch of his hand.

He briefly 'saw' the other possibility, where he didn't detonate the bomb, where those lives—but then he 'saw' the explosion happening anyway and he understood.

He was hungry. The food the girls were eating smelled so good.

He smiled at them and they glanced at each other, confused.

Lukas took his hand out of the pocket. He ripped the coat off, exposing the vest. One of the girls at the table screamed. They were scrambling away. There were shouts, but they were far away, not in the near bubble of consciousness. He reached into one of the many slots on the vest and found the old-style flip phone.

Screams, yelling, someone running toward him, arms stretched wide to wrap around him, the correct response to a suicide bomber, one the Israelis had learned at great cost.

Lukas slid the phone out, saw the wires connecting it to the vest, pulled them free, and then put it on the table, just as it vibrated from an incoming call.

He had another moment of clarity and he 'saw' her. He finally had a glimpse of the reason why he was here, not *this* here exactly, but in the now. He had to get to *her*. The *We*.

"I'm hungry," Lukas said, reaching across the table for an abandoned falafel, a moment before he was swarmed under.

Lara's Journal

"There is no such thing as complete consciousness." Julian Jaynes

WELL, THAT WAS HARDER THAN I thought, which is sorta weird cause I can't remember hard or harder or what I thought. But, whatever my expectation was, it was based on the brain I got. Which, according to Dr. Jenkins's diagnosis, has a few screws loose and some broken—yeah, maybe she's right about that. Just the brain part. She says I was concussed and suffered from a hematoma, which leaked into my temporal lobe. I know where that lobe is cause it's behind the twenty staples in my head and the way huger chunk of hair they shaved off for that.

I'm wearing a Red Sox cap and you don't even want to know what I had to do to get that. But, any girl, no matter the age, looks a bit odd with a chunk of skull shaved and shiny staples in her head. I was gonna wait till they took the staples out to break as free,. but, they were gonna move me to a place where there would be no getting out of, so Lara took a chance. Lily would still be sitting in that room waiting to be transferred to the Fourth Floor. But, I'm not her. I don't know who I am—but, I sure as shit ain't her. And I sure as shit ain't going to the Fourth Floor, whatever that is.

Really, a little sister, a little brother? Wouldn't you remember them or have some ache of missing them? Something? Dr. Jenkins says their names were Sarah and George. Yeah, right you can name a baby Lily, but you fall back to George?

I don't think so.

But, I could be wrong. Maybe I did kill them.

Maybe that person, that memory was in that part of my brain that got concussed and bled.

Oddly enough, I can buy into that easier than I'd ever wear that shirt.

So, I need to write down how I got away because I can't trust my own mind, which would be rather gross to people who do trust theirs but once you don't—it's not so bad.

It seems I have something that makes people do things. No, not like that with my body, but with my brain, which is missing a piece underneath

the shaved off hair and staples. Or maybe I could always do it? I edge people who are inclined the right way. Which means looking at a skinny sixteen-year-old girl with some semblance of tits and—okay, so yeah that way, but not all the way. They just think they are, but they aren't. Doesn't make sense to me either, but it works. Of course, I could be missing something in that, since I'm missing a whole lot before that.

Mike the night guy—yeah, that was easy and it came to me like riding a bike. Not sure I can ride a bike but I edged Mike to the point where I am here.

Actually, I had to edge two more guys and I do believe that men working in a lock down mental institution shouldn't cough up freedom as easily as I did that. I don't think Lily could have done that—but, Lara could. It's just another reason that I know I'm not Lily with her murdered family—you don't do what I'm willing to do and then just kill people. It makes no sense. Why would you resort to killing when you obviously have so many other talents to get what you want?

So, now I'm in this diner with my cap, watching the guy behind the counter named Joey, cut pies. I know that's his name because it's sewn onto his blue shirt just above the left pocket. He holds a big knife and it grosses me out to even look at him cutting through pecans and the rest. Really, did I use a knife like that to kill my whole family, the family I can't remember?

I don't think so.

But, now I'm, Lara, on my own. I have eight dollars. I'm only having coffee, so that's OK. I think it's a hard thing to be me in a sweatshirt that says Troy State and some jeans that are not that much different than Lily's jeans cause that's what Mike provided, which was much nicer than the other two guards who merely turned a key for my edge.

The eight dollars I stole off a girl in the common room. They were paying her to eat. It wasn't working.

She'll be in there till her heart eats itself. Sorta stupid but that's gonna happen whether I took her eight bucks or not. And I just heard some guy talking and I'm in Boise. Not quite sure where that is but I can pretend all day long. The last place I knew about was Wichita. I read that upside down in Dr. Jenkins's file while she talked on the phone. The file said I was from Wichita? No, I don't think so, cause my immediate thought was who the hell lives in Wichita? See? That shouldn't be my first thought if Wichita was home. Should it? Is there even a George Washington High School in Wichita?

If I had a cell phone, I could Google that.

Guess I could ask someone who has a phone to do it, but really, wouldn't you think it odd if some random girl sitting in a diner asked you to do Google something?

I'm writing and watching Joey cut those pies and I know with all my heart that I couldn't stab anyone fifty-four times with a knife like that. Especially not my little brother.

But, I don't have a little brother and have never had a little brother—Lily did.

You okay, kid? *And that's Joey, noticing me, which could be a good thing or a bad thing. Depends if I want some pie.*

I don't think so.

He's one of those guys, the ones you don't notice, but actually he's kind of good looking, although he's not very big. But he moves so smoothly, there's something about it. And he's looking at me as I write and it's like I'm the only person in the universe to him.

I'm fine

I can tell he doesn't believe me. But at least he isn't trying to see what I'm writing. Yeah, I write the words, because I want to remember it all.

You all alone?

I don't like that question. Aren't we all?

He raises an eyebrow, not impressed with my witty philosophical repartee. I'm not really either; it's just what came to me.

A girl like you shouldn't be all alone.

What the hell does that mean? I'm all right. *What kind of girl am I like?*

He frowns, but then his attention shifts past me so I guess I'm not that interesting after all. I look where he's looking to see what's more interesting than me and it's just an old, white-haired woman sitting in a corner booth, wearing a black raincoat, slowly stirring a spoon in a cup of tea. She has on sunglasses, which doesn't seem to make sense given the raincoat. Seriously?

He shifts back to me and grins. Okey-dokey, kid. You want some pie?

And I almost hurl, thinking about the way he was using that knife, and shake my head. No, thanks.

Two bucks, then, for the coffee.

I peel them off, consider a tip, consider it's all I got, and leave the two. It doesn't seem to bother Joey. And really, it isn't like this is Starbucks. Two dollars for coffee?

I gotta go thumb a ride. Another edge--seems to be my fate in this world I've known since last Tuesday.

And I only got six bucks.

As I'm folding these pages to leave, Joey says: Be safe, kid.

Really?

But I pause before quitting writing—Joey reminds me of someone. A boyfriend from George Washington High in Wichita? But he's too old.

Time to go.

* * *

OMG—I didn't have to do a thing for that ride except listen to Johnny Cash over and over. When he pulled over, he said, Hey cutie where you going, *and I didn't know so I said,* Wherever you are.

He was a nice enough guy in a nice enough car and I thought I'd have to edge for sure. But, all he wanted was companionship. When he said it, I realized that I didn't quite remember that word; it's lost under the staples. But, I think it means that my just being there is enough. He drove through a lotta dark and I feel asleep listening to Johnny Cash sing: I hurt myself today *and some part of me did understand that enough to fall asleep without all the pills they used to give me.*

When I woke up we were stopped and he said, I gotta drop you here cutie cause I'm home.

Where is here? I asked, looking out into the rainy morning that I'm still sitting in.

The Dalles.

I had to wonder what kind of place has 'The' before it. Like there was A Dalles?

He musta saw the look on my face. Biggest town in Oregon after Portland.

Apparently, my look needed more as he expanded his description:

Bobbie the Wonder Dog passed through here in 1924, *he added, most unhelpfully except to let me know not much happening The Dalles. Not lately.*

I'll have to Google that little tidbit some day.

If I remember, which isn't likely, but I'm writing it down so, maybe.

At least I know what state I'm in and it's not Kansas. Or Boise, except that's not a state and I'm trying to remember what state, but drawing a blank right now.

He gave me forty dollars and said, Good luck.

So, I got forty-eight dollars. Forty-six minus two for coffee, but I'm not so sure about the luck. It's raining. I found a bus stop with a cover so I'm writing here with the rain pouring down without touching me. It's sorta like all of this world not touching me. I don't know where I'm going. I just know I have to go somewhere. A truck just pulled up—a big one going to big places. I don't like him cause I know I'm gonna probably have to edge.

He has that need all above his head, like that cloud of dirt that used to follow that dirty kid in Snoopy, except this is much dirtier, but he has a bed above that cab and I want a bed more than anything right now. Maybe that's how I lived before. Just making stuff work.

He's getting irritated that I'm not hopping in, that I'm still writing.

But the writing is important. I gotta remember.

If I did kill my family—I know I can handle him. I just want to sleep and wake up and be Lara who just had the worst nightmare ever.

* * *

OK that was a nightmare, but I'm in Portland, rather on the outside of Portland and I'm writing this before I sleep so I can remember when I wake, because otherwise it will all be gone wherever everything else in my past has gone.

I'm pretty sure that I've never been here before. I'd feel something about this place, but there is nothing familiar at all.

Jake, the guy driving that truck. I was asleep on that nice long bed where you can stretch out and I was dreaming that a lion was staring at me. He grabbed me with his claws, I could feel them sink into my forearms and see the blood, then I woke up, and Jake was on top of me with his hands holding down my arms, his nails in that same part of my forearms as the lion in the dream.

The weird part is that I couldn't remember if I knew this feeling or not. This total invasion of me; was it something new or familiar? I looked into his eyes and said Jake, "if you want me, wouldn't you like me to be here with you?"

He pulled away. That seemed to be familiar, so, either a lot of guys had attacked me while I was asleep, or I knew how to make them go away without edging. I wasn't sure about either one but preferred the latter cause it made me feel stronger. More like the Lara who'd never wear that shirt.

He stuffed twenty bucks in my hand and shoved me out into the rain near the rest stop that read twenty miles to Portland. So, I got 66 bucks and at this rate—I might make it. I put the twenty in the pocket of Mike's cruddy jeans. Yeah, dripping wet in five seconds. That's how much Portland sucks. Or twenty miles away. Maybe the city was some lovely dry mirage twenty miles from here and then I thought—mirage, I know that.

I stuck out my thumb cause the bus never comes and that's how I met Martha. Now, at the end of this most strange day, I kinda wonder why she stopped for me. It doesn't seem in her nature, but maybe a dripping wet girl sorta sixteen, but really older, hitching in the rain appealed to her. If

I'd known what I think she's really like, now after knowing her some more hours, because there is something odd about her and her husband—I might not have jumped into that Honda, but she was there and I was out in the rain and she didn't have dick and need edging so I was good.

She asked, Where are you going?

And I just fessed up cause really, why lie now? I said, I don't know.

She asked, Are the cops after you?

And I said. No they are not, *cause the last I knew—guards were after me, not cops.*

She seemed OK with that and said Where's home?

Since Jake's semi-bed was my last home I said: I was attacked there. I just want to be anywhere that isn't there.

She asked, How old are you?

And I said, Twenty-two.

She asked, What's your name?

And I said, Lily Crand.

Some part of me must have touched her own DNA and she said, I'll take you to my home and we'll figure it out from there.

Great, I was all in. Fuck me stupid. Home is twenty miles into Portland, twenty more miles out of Portland on road that got narrower and narrower between the biggest trees I'd ever seen. More like a tunnel. The road turned to gravel and could fit only one car. I started to worry about never coming back through this forest. Isn't Oregon home to serial killers? Or gives birth to them or something?

I'll have to Google that. When I can Google.

She pulled up to a gate set in a twelve-foot high fence that stretched into the forest left and right as far as I could see. I mean a real gate where she pushed a button on her visor and it slid open, then slid shut behind us without her doing a thing. I know cause I looked back. Even her driveway was long. A long way from the gate to one big garage that could fit four cars. That forest inside the fence is perfect. Perfect grass, perfect ferns, which I seemed to recognize, and just perfect everything. It was Disneyland if one person could claim it. The wild forest had given away to something inside that fence, something that had tamed it and shaped it. And something about that bothers me.

I got no idea how I know what Disneyland is but I do and I file it away with sorta knowing what being attacked feels like although you don't remember. By the time we got to what she called home, I sorta liked her because she didn't talk. She didn't ask me anything or chatter on about bullshit like guys do while you're edging them. She was like me, just living in the moment and was taking me home. Maybe I should have pondered on that a bit, but I didn't. I do now but not then and here I am, so does it even matter? Is this place any worse than any other place?

It appears a lot better.

Definitely better than Jake's truck.

It's the biggest house I've ever seen. I knew that as we pulled up even though I couldn't remember if I'd seen bigger. I just knew that neither Lily nor Lara had been in a place like this. She pushed another button and one of the four garage doors slid open and the lights all came on and the only thing in the garage was a convertible something that I didn't recognize and a pick up truck. That was it. Not one rake, or hoe, or other crud you don't need in the house anymore and move into the garage. That's what I first saw and I probably shoulda walked that long driveway back onto the gravel road. But, I didn't. Because where then? The wild forest?

I was starving and while I did notice the perfectly painted walls and baseboards that looked like someone had spent days with a toothbrush there, all I wanted was some food and my own toothbrush...for my teeth. In the halogen brightness of that perfect garage some guy walks in and Martha says. Oh, there's Jake.

Really? His name is Jake?

That hurt my stomach.

She looks at Jake and says, This is Lily, she's a lost soul for a moment and we're gonna help her with that" *and he looks at me with the same dead eyes that the first Jake had and was blasting through me when I woke up with him on top of me. I knew it wasn't gonna be good. But, I'm a lost soul. What choice do I have?*

The sandwich would have been better with real bread. Martha asked if I was gluten free. Maybe I am, but right now, I'd be happy knowing my birthday and eating anything, even gluten. It's a nice kitchen, one for looking at and admiring and not really cooking. I don't know how I know that. Very strange what you do remember when you don't remember who you are.

Jake came in carrying a big cell phone and held it in front of me and said, Nice Facebook page, Lily Cole. *And there it is: Lily Cole.*

Lot's of selfies, I seem to be rather interested in myself, and I have 22 friends. I wonder if they miss me? I read some of the comments. Nice butt got five likes. The last one says 'where are you?' And I think at least someone misses me and then I see it's from Dr. Jenkins. Did they just leave my page up from before? Wouldn't they take it down when they locked me up in that place? There's also nothing about murdering my family, although I guess that's not something you update your own page with. I'm not sure who I am or what's going on and now I'm starting to doubt everything.

Martha doesn't ask about the last name, which is weird, as weird as the look Jake is giving me.

I'm getting a headache. I drink five glasses of water and still feel thirsty. Martha takes me to a guest room that's so inviting, I wonder how she ever gets anyone out of it, but maybe she rarely let's anyone into it? But I'm here, so why would I think that?

She hands me one of Jake's T-shirts from a laundry room and says, Take a nice shower and get some sleep and we'll all talk on this in the morning.

Talk on what? But suddenly I'm tired. Jake is still staring at his phone and glancing over at me as if to confirm it's me. Martha pushes him out the door and says, Good night, *and pulls the door shut behind her. I reach over and lock it.*

It takes me ten minutes to get the cover and all the extra pillows off the bed. The bed isn't really intended for sleeping. Well not till you purge it down to the sheets and one thin blanket. And the sheets feel scratchy. Obviously, I'm used to a higher thread count. How can you know nothing about yourself but remember something as mundane as the thread count of sheets? And why would a house this big and fancy have cheap sheets in the guest room?

Just before I fall asleep, I drag myself into the bathroom to pee. The water is going through me fast. Not like it had a lot of bread to work through. I notice I squat daintily over what is obviously the cleanest toilet within miles and miles, although it didn't look like there was anything within miles and miles. I guess I'm not a toilet seat sitter.

It doesn't square up with how easily I fell into edging. I could add it to a list of what doesn't square up, but it would be a long list and it's hard enough writing all this stuff down so I can remember.

I'm beginning to think I'm an odd duck. Not the sorta feeling you want to have about yourself when today is the first day you actually have what is in your head written down on paper. There's a little card with perfect calligraphy, set on a gold stand resting on the toilet tank, which reads: Please, nothing but toilet paper. Septic tank.

I'm suddenly filled with a desire to shove my shoes into the toilet. I am an odd duck. Seems I don't like rules. I wipe from front to back so I know that. I flush and the toilet barely makes a small gurgle. I wash my hands and open one of the drawers and there's a pack of new toothbrushes like you get at Costco. Suddenly, I can see one of those warehouse stores in the galling emptiness of my own mind. It's the first thing I've really seen in my mind's eye that I'm pretty sure was real before today. I brush my teeth in a very organized fashion. Thirty seconds on each quarter of my teeth. I wonder how many people have ever felt so strange brushing their teeth.

I'm counting the time in my head before I switch to the other side and seem to know to massage my gums gently.

I turn off the lights except the one on the table next to the bed and crawl into the scratchy sheets. and I think I might have been a promiscuous dental hygienist with really good linens.

I don't pray. An agnostic promiscuous dental hygienist maybe?

I pulled the Ziploc bag out and here I am now, up to date, near as I can remember, which is never really good, but that's a pretty good accounting of today.

And now I will stop writing and am afraid I will fall into the deepest sleep ever, but who knows what my deepest sleep was?

I just know I need sleep, even though I'm terrified of my dreams.

How screwed is that?

Black Site, The Negev Desert, Israel

"Our sense of justice depends on our sense of time. Justice is a phenomenon only of consciousness, because time spread out in spatial succession is its very essence." Julian Jaynes

LUKAS WAS NAKED AND COLD, his first awareness as he regained consciousness. Naked, which should be bad, was good, because it meant he wasn't wearing the bomb. Cold was cold, a simple reality of the here and now. It didn't bother him much.

Most of all he was still really hungry.

As awareness rose in his mind. He knew he was in a vehicle. Movement along with engine and tire noise, indicated that. He was sitting in car, someone on either side.

He didn't open his eyes, letting his other senses explore first.

His hands were cuffed. He knew this because he felt the tight, cold steel digging into his wrists. It hurt, but distantly.

A seat belt was around his waist. He lurched forward as the vehicle came to an abrupt halt. He heard voices, but couldn't make out what they were saying.

He opened his eyes to blackness. A hood.

The vehicle accelerated, but they only drove for a minute before stopping again.

"I know you are conscious," the person to his left said. He hit Lukas in the side, a short jab into the ribs, but focused with years of training and a rib cracked with an audible snap. The man on the right gave a snort of approval as Lukas gasped in pain.

A gloved hand slid across his naked belly and pressed the release for the seatbelt. Car doors opened and hands grabbed him. He was yanked out, lifted between the two men and carried, toes barely touching a concrete floor.

He sensed the men carrying him were dark mirrors. Empty spaces where their humanity should be. The place emitted more emotion than them, but Lukas didn't want to focus on that, because the place had the ugliest aura he'd ever experienced. He was certain of that even though he couldn't remember much before the marketplace, but it was uglier than the dark cellar he could remember and that had been a bad place with bad people, especially the whisperer.

Despair, fear, hopelessness, anger, shame, disgust, and a swirl of the place's aura that Lukas's mind shied away from. He put a mental wall between him and the place.

Another door opened with a screech of metal protesting metal, and then he was tossed, tumbling on to a cold, concrete floor. The metal shrieked again and the door slammed shut.

"Who's there?" Lukas asked as collected himself and sat up, registering the pain from the broken rib. He held up his hands. "Can you take these off?"

Not emptiness. Utter blackness, which is different than the empty space of the two men. This was an absorption of all around it.

"No."

A woman.

Lukas reached up and tugged the sack off his head, tossing it aside. It was dim, a faint trace of light coming from a four-inch square hole in the ceiling. Lukas stared at it. A shaft through the concrete roof, the light so faint that if he hadn't been in complete darkness for so long, he wouldn't be able to see anything.

Still, it was light. Sunlight, bouncing its way in through a narrow shaft in many feet of reinforced concrete.

Reluctantly, Lukas lowered his gaze. A woman dressed in khaki pants and long sleeve shirt sat on a wooden chair, to one side of the door. She wore a black balaclava, ice blue eyes peering out of black holes. Thin pale sliver lips in the dark opening for a mouth; that was the only flesh she had exposed as she also wore black gloves.

Lukas met her gaze and held it. Not challenging, just accepting. Neither blinked.

"Why didn't you detonate the vest?" the woman finally asked.

Lukas didn't answer.

"Why did you remove the wires from the phone?"

Lukas remained quiet.

"How did you know the phone was in the vest and wired to remotely detonate it?"

The silence lasted minutes.

"Being naked doesn't bother you." The woman made it a statement. "It's usually the first crack. Especially when a man realizes they're being watched by a woman."

"Is that why you're in here?" Lukas asked.

She ignored the question. "My associates think you didn't detonate because you valued your life. That you were afraid to die. That's what the others we've captured finally admit. That is what they want me to get you to admit. That when it came to it, you were a coward. We could get you to say it. We could get you to say anything we want. Whether it is true or not. I prefer true."

The woman rubbed the fingers of her right hand on the fingers of her left with a slight squeak of leather.

"But if you valued your life," the woman continued, "you would have tried to get away. Not sit down at a table and reveal the vest. That made no sense. Someone said you were asking for food."

"I did. I'm hungry. Could—"

"Shut up."

"I didn't hurt anyone."

"You could have killed dozens with the amount of explosives and shrapnel in that vest."

"But as you note, I didn't."

The woman was silent for a few moment, cold eyes staring at him. "Why didn't you detonate the vest?"

"Life," Lukas said. "I could feel the life all around me."

The first color touched the black surrounding the woman. A brief flash of purple. "'Feel'? What do you mean?"

Lukas shrugged. "We were all one. I could kill me, but I couldn't kill them. That is not for me to decide."

She snorted in disgust. "Who gets to decide life and death?"

"Fate," Lukas said. He frowned, something flitting at the edges of his gray memory, something beyond the immediate past.

"'Fate'?" The woman's voice was full of scorn. "What is fate?"

"Who is Fate," Lukas automatically corrected, a piece falling into place. "The three. Clotho spins. Lachesis measures. Atropos cuts."

"What are you talking about?"

"I don't know," Lukas said. "But when you asked, that answer came."

"I thought you couldn't remember."

"Your question drew forth the answer."

"But not the answer I want."

"I gave you an answer to the question you asked," Lukas said, in a reasonable tone, as if they were discussing this over coffee in a café.

The woman didn't feel the same way. "Why did you go there wearing the vest?"

"It is what they wanted."

"Your cell. Your fellow terrorists. Don't pretend you aren't one of them."

Lukas tried to remember the faces in the dark cellar. He smiled.

"What is so funny?" the woman demanded, another flash of purple tinged with red.

"Their place was not much different than this place. It felt the same."

"Not 'their' place," the woman corrected. "Your place. You were one of them. *Are* one of them."

"I don't know who I am. I don't know who they were."

"That's a new one," the woman said. "Don't worry. We'll help you remember who you are. We'll soon know more about you than you can ever remember about yourself."

"That won't be hard," Lukas said, "since I hardly remember anything."

"I agree. It won't be hard. For me, that is. For you, it will be as hard you make it."

Lukas didn't say anything.

"We are the best in the world," the woman said, "at extracting information. We also have the best network in the world for gathering intelligence. We will know who you are soon enough."

Lukas nodded. "That would be good."

"Don't take an attitude like that," the woman warned. "Attitudes get crushed here."

Lukas had nothing to say to that.

"How did you know about the phone?" the woman asked again. "When they don't trust the bomber, they hide a phone in the vest, wired to the detonator. In case someone does what you did. But the phone was booby-trapped. A trap within a trap. How did you know it was there? How did you know how to disarm it?"

"I don't know."

"Troops are scouring the area for your handler. The one who called to detonate when he saw that you had chickened out. He had to be in visual contact with you. You do realize he was going to kill you?"

"Since it seems I was going to kill me, I can't really hold that against whoever it was."

"He didn't trust you."

"Obviously, he was right."

"Give me his name."

"I don't know."

"What is *your* name?" the woman asked. "We're running your fingerprints. Along with facial recognition and DNA. We'll know, so withholding it is only a speed bump."

"Lukas."

"Spell it."

Lukas did so.

"And your last name?"

"I don't know."

Another flash of emotion, more red than purple. "Speed bumps can painful."

"I can't tell you what I don't know."

"Now you're going to tell me you were brainwashed? That they wiped out your memories somehow? That you had no volition? A Manchurian Candidate?"

"I don't know any of that. Do you have a name? I gave you mine."

"You don't ask questions."

"It would make conversing easier."

The woman canted her head, looking down at him as if he were some curious animal that had entered her personal domain. "You're very strange."

"Are you supposed to be the nice one?" Lukas asked. He nodded toward a small black orb in one corner of the cell, barely visible in the low light. "The other one, the one who will really hurt me, he's watching isn't he?"

She didn't look at the camera. "I am Rahel."

Lukas nodded. "Rahel."

"You speak English," Rahel said something in Hebrew and he looked at her blankly. She switched back to English. "Your accent is almost American. Not British. Where are you from?"

"I don't know."

"You're young. A boy. You knew you were expendable putting that vest on. The homicide vest. If it were actually a suicide vest, little fucks like you would put it on, walk into the middle of the desert and blow themselves up. When you kill others, it's homicide."

Lukas saw red blossom around Rahel. "I am sorry."

She stood, walked over to him. "'Sorry'? You are going to be very, very sorry. You're going to wish you'd pushed the detonator."

"I'm sorry about your husband and your son," Lukas said.

Rahel took a step back. "What? What did you say?"

"I'm sorry they were killed. It was wrong. What I was going to do was wrong. That's why I didn't do it. No one should do that. It's not human. No one should do what you're doing in this place. It's not human, either."

Rahel's voice went up a notch. "'Human'? What do you know of human? You're the one who was wearing the bomb!" She kicked, a heavy, steel-toed boot, catching Lukas in the solar plexus, knocking the wind out of him, a spike of pain from the broken rib adding to the agony. Lukas curled into a ball as more kicks followed.

His mind floated away from his body.

The door opened and several men ran in, grabbing Rahel, pulling her away and out, the door clanging shut behind.

Lukas preferred to remain where he was, somewhere not here, not quite sure where.

Lara

"The language of men was involved with only one hemisphere in order to leave the other free for the language of the Gods." **Julian Jaynes**

I KNOW I'M DREAMING, but that doesn't mean much. I'm dreaming that I'm in this bed, that I hear whispering outside the door. It sounds like Jake, Martha's Jake, but the other voice is another man. I know I'm dreaming because I have to pee again and the toilet is the same one as in the institution, right here in the cell with my bed. I sit on the toilet and when I flush, there's the huge whooshing of an industrial toilet and not the nice one from earlier. I bet you could put anything in this toilet and the system would take it. Even my shoes, but they're actually slippers, not the shoes I was wearing when I escaped.

For some reason, the cheap slippers bum me out more than the cell.

I still hear the whispering, but the whole room is now the institution cell. I don't like this dream and fall into bed. The sheets are even cheaper. I fall back asleep in my dream, which is a weird feeling let me tell you, and suddenly I'm in a long hallway. Stark white tile floors and walls. There's a pay phone on the far wall. It begins to ring and I run toward it, but it's one of those awful dreams where the faster you run the farther away everything gets.

I want to wake up. I look up as if awake is some place above my head and if I could just reach it and pull myself to consciousness I'd be fine. I start to panic. What if I can't wake up? What if this isn't a dream? What if I'm in a coma or something and I'm stuck in this white hallway forever with the phone ringing?

But then it's gone and I'm in the kitchen again, not Martha's kitchen, the other one, and that is absolutely where I do not want to be. Not again. Seems if you really, really, want to wake up, no matter how bad what you're waking up to is, you oughta be able. But I can't. I see the blood trail out the door of the kitchen to the rest of the house where I can't go, the bloody knife in my hand, and now that corridor and that phone I can't reach is such a better option and then I'm there, running and suddenly I'm at the phone and reach for the receiver. I don't ever call on a phone though,

22

I think I text. I know that the same way I know how to brush my teeth because it's the real me but I grab this old phone and listen. Its Dr. Jenkins and she's saying, *Lily, wake up.*

I'm so relieved to be told to wake up that I grab onto the dream-line. I open my eyes and I'm staring at the white acoustic tiles of the institution cell. I feel the thin mattress under me, so different from that thick, plush Tempurpedic I fell asleep on. I turn a bit and see Dr. Jenkins's concerned face.

You were having a nightmare, Lily.

I take her hand. *"Did I edge anyone?*

What are you talking about?

And I'm so relieved not to be in that kitchen that I don't mind waking up back here. She hands me a small cup of water, the paper sort that look likes what you'd wrap around an ice cream cone, and I notice the bottom is leaking a steady drip, drip.

She gives me a pill and says: *Take this. It'll relax you.*

And I do because relaxing would be nice, except I remember right after taking it where relaxing leads, but it's too late.

I fall back asleep, but I hear her lock the door from the outside, and then the gentle tap of her low heels on highly buffed linoleum. But then the heels get louder and I wonder if she's walking in a circle outside my door but then the tap becomes a rap and another, a bit louder, and another even louder and I open my eyes and I'm in Martha's guest room.

The expensive mattress is cradling me in the cheap sheets. Someone's knocking on the door.

Lily? Lily? It's noon. The maids are here. They need to clean the room. Martha's voice is urgent, as if I'm breaking a rule that I should have known about.

I drag myself from the bed feeling as though I did just take a pill to make me relax and trudge through the thick carpet, feeling lost inside of Jake's huge shirt and even more lost inside a labyrinth most people just call their mind. I open the door and Martha gives a forced smile.

You missed breakfast but I'm making lunch. My, you don't look that well rested for someone who just slept fifteen hours. Were you awake all night?

No, I mutter. *I fell asleep as soon as I hit the bed—both of them.*

She looks at me strangely or more strangely than she has which is a weird thing to do when you pick up a stranger and bring them home. *I dreamt I was back in the institution.*

An Institution, she says her eyes widening with some late coming alarm. She says it with a capital I, which it doesn't deserve.

I hear banging noises and she says, *oh that's the maids. They are so rough on things.*

She goes into the hallway to give some strict instructions in a tone that makes it very clear that she's done this many times before.

But the banging doesn't stop and then I hear the noise of that key and I wake up and turn over and some man says, "Breakfast," with a complete lack of enthusiasm.

Suddenly I'm wide-awake and do feel rested as if I slept fifteen hours and through the open door I see Mike with his cart in the hallway and there's a tray on the table near the door.

"Am I dreaming you?" I say because I'm not quite sure about anything right now and feel so lonely and lost and notice I can still feel the damp spot on the thin blanket from the leaking cup.

Mike pauses in his noise making and looks in. "I hope you're dreaming this breakfast tray because this oatmeal looks like cement."

I'm suddenly so happy to be where I know I am because the oatmeal here *is* like cement. It was like cement yesterday. After he leaves, I wolf it down as if it were the finest mush from the Ritz. I think I'm getting better and I finally have a real dream to tell Dr. Jenkins.

Mike takes my empty tray and says, "well, you're getting your appetite back. That's good but it doesn't seem too discriminating so maybe not so good."

I tell him, "Thanks. When will Doctor Jenkins come?"

As he's carrying the tray and fumbling with his keys he says, "Doctor Jenkins?"

Fuck. "My Doctor?"

"Jacobson is your doctor."

Oh, of course Jake. "Who is Doctor Jenkins?" I wonder aloud.

He looks worried. "Your doctor is Jacobson. Must be tough to have scrambled eggs inside of that head of yours. You don't want Jenkins as your doctor. That's a whole different ball of wax, kid."

Really? You think? A ball of wax?

I curl back on the bed and pull up the blanket, which seems to be the only thing I took with me in my dream to Martha's house. It was so real; I had to have been there.

Mike says, "You should get dressed and come out to the commons. It's not good to lie around too much."

Mike seems to have a real gift for stating the obvious.

"Get dressed and I'll be back in ten." He locks the door.

I go to pee and I'm sitting on the seat before I remember that I'm a squatter. I lift up a bit and my thighs start to scream and I think, no I'm a sitter. I hear the roar of the flush and wash my hands and look in the mirror. The girl looking back at me isn't the one from the Facebook page. Her hair was shorter and blonder, except where the staples are. The eyes are sorta the same and maybe the teeth. We obviously both brush well. I turn and look at my butt; really, only five likes?

I go to the metal closet and pull out a T-shirt and some jeans. The T-shirt is like the one Martha handed me, but my size, not hanging to my knees. I wonder how I could have imagined that little calligraphy note and not have come up with some silk pajamas or something. I remember Martha's bed cover and thousand throw pills but couldn't conjure up anything better than a longer version of this shirt? For some reason that makes me even sadder which is saying a lot about yourself when you have no memory and it seems you killed your family. You wouldn't think a girl capable of that would brush her teeth so perfectly for two solid minutes. I'm only in the jeans holding my bra and that shirt when the door opens again. Mike's eyes linger on my breasts for a few seconds too long and he doesn't turn away or blush.

I suddenly remember he had pulled at my nipples while I was edging him, and for a moment I stare at him and try to remember if that actually happened, and if it did, what did I really do? But, I can't read anything in his face beyond the fact that he might give me a like for my tits.

Black Site, The Negev Desert, Israel

"We have to face the fact that modern man suffers from a kind of poverty of the spirit, which stands in glaring contrast with a scientific and technological abundance." **Martin Luther King Jr.**

HEAVY METAL MUSIC THUMPED through the thick concrete walls of Lukas's cell. He was cold, but not too cold. He had a feeling everything about this place was calculated. From the temperature to the music. All with one purpose: to destroy a person's self. He tried to understand what kind of human would sit down and design such a facility with such a goal?

A clever person, for certain. A cold person, also for certain.

He was even hungrier, which he wouldn't have thought was possible.

He had no idea how long he'd been here. He'd had to piss and had crawled over the four inch hole in the floor which was covered a mesh grate. Other than that, nothing had happened except the music, which had started a little while ago.

How long was a little while?

The door swung open, hinges protesting and it occurred to Lukas that someone went out of their way to insure they made that noise, when any reasonable person would have sprayed a dab of oil. He wondered if they had a hinge guy, who went around, checking them, making sure they were bone-dry with just the right amount of friction and rust.

Two men wheeled in a gurney. He didn't know if they were the same from the car, but they felt the same. Empty.

One pulled a Taser from a pocket and aimed it at him.

"I'll cooper—" he began, but then the dart hit him, the electricity jolted down the wires, and he spasmed on the floor. While he was helpless, they tossed him on the gurney, uncuffed him, and secured his ankles and wrists, along with straps across his knees, waist, and chest.

When they were done, the electricity had dissipated, and he was secured horizontally on the gurney. He had to admit he was impressed with their efficiency; they must have a lot of practice strapping people to gurneys.

They rolled him out of the room and down a dim corridor lined with concrete walls painted dull gray. A rusty door screeched ahead, or was it afoot, of him.

There was a bump as he was rolled into a room with the same gray, concrete walls. Except this one had a light instead of a hole in the roof. A bright light, too powerful to look at directly. Lukas appreciated its warmth. He was placed in the center and the wheels were locked down. The two men left, but Lukas knew he wasn't alone.

"Are you feeling better?" Lukas asked.

"How did you know about me?" Rahel asked.

"You told me."

"I didn't tell you anything about myself," Rahel said.

"I thought you had." Lukas turned his head. Rahel was standing to his left, still wearing the mask. There was a flat screen TV mounted on a cart next to her. "Are you no longer considered the nice one because you beat me?"

"What I did was nothing," she said. "There is much worse ahead of you unless you cooperate."

"I would like to cooperate," Lukas said. "Why do you hide?"

"You don't ask questions," the woman said. "You answer them."

"Can I have something to eat?"

"You don't listen very well," the woman said.

Lukas closed his eyes.

"You have no record," she said. "No facial profiling, fingerprints, none of it comes up."

"So you have no answers," Lukas said.

"We're waiting on the DNA." She indicated the TV. "It's up to you whether you wish to remain silent. We found your friends."

"I don't think they were my friends," Lukas said. "I don't know how I ended up with them. What do they say about me?" He actually wanted to know.

A hesitation. "They lie."

"What lie did they tell about me?"

"Is that all you're concerned about?" Rahel demanded. "Yourself?"

"I cannot know about others until I know myself."

"Stop the cheap philosophy. You pretended to know something about me."

"You showed me that. There was no pretense. I'm sorry."

"Stop saying that." She turned to the TV and pushed a button. The screen flickered. The image was black and white. A man on a gurney, like Lukas, in a similar room. "Your cell leader."

"I remember the face," Lukas said. "He told me what to do."

"And you were going to do it."

"But I didn't."

Rahel snorted. "Watch. This is your future. This is my not-nice associate."

A man wearing a black mask appeared, leaning over the body on the gurney. He had a prod in one hand. He pressed it against the prone man's body. There was no sound, but the cell leader's mouth was wide, silently screaming. His body writhed.

Again and again the prod was applied.

"That may be my future, but it is his past," Lukas said after twenty seconds.

"What?"

"He's already dead," Lukas said.

Rahel turned from the screen to him. "He's not."

"That is a recording. He's dead."

"How do you know that?"

"I can't feel him."

Rahel turned the TV off. She grabbed the wooden chair, turned its back to him and straddled it, adjacent to his head. "They said you just walked into their safe house. That they should have killed you. They thought you were working for Mossad or CIA or the Jordanians. How else would you know where they were? But you weren't armed or wired. You only knew your name. You volunteered to die. The game you are playing with me; they say you played with them. But how could you have known where they were?"

"Can I have something to eat?" Lukas asked.

"I think you are much more than you appear to be," the woman said.

"What do I appear to be?"

"You pretend to be a young fool. To know nothing. But your actions say you know much. You knew the location of their safe house. How? You know about my family. How? None of it makes sense." She shook her head. "Unfortunately for you, I must make sense of it."

"I would help you, if I could."

"I don't understand why you allowed them to put the vest on you. Why you went to the market."

"The '*We*' was greater than the I," Lukas said.

"What does that mean?"

"I did what they wanted me to do."

"Not all the way."

"*The 'We'* changed. Once I was among other people, I did what was best for them."

Rahel shook her head. "You make no sense."

"I'm sorry."

"Don't say that." Rahel sighed. "You said something earlier. 'Clotho spins. Lachesis measures. Atropos cuts.' I looked it up. Those are the three Fates. Also known as the Moirai, from ancient Greece. Legends. Myths. Not reality."

"What of your faith?" Lukas asked. "One who is not of the same faith would believe the same about it. A myth."

"You're saying you believe in these Fates of legend?" Rahel asked. "That they are real to you?"

Lukas shrugged. "I don't know. You asked a question about who decides who dies and those names came to me."

"So you do have more in your memory than you pretend."

"I am not pretending."

Rahel shook her head. "We don't have time to play games. For me to ask a thousand questions in order to get answers. Especially answers that are gibberish."

"But you looked up the names," Lukas pointed out.

"How old are you?" Rahel asked.

Lukas frowned. "I don't know."

"You are not an innocent," Rahel said. "I can look at you and see that."

"What do you mean?"

Rahel walked over. She undid the strap around his chest and arms. Then began to tap his flesh as she pointed. "Knife wound here. Another here, long slice, badly healed. Puncture wound here, although not a bullet, more an arrow or spear according to our doctor. Your hands have many small scars, consistent with martial arts. Defense wounds on your palms and forearms. All healed, some well, some poorly."

Lukas lifted his head, following as she pointed out these marks.

"For someone so young," Rahel said, "you have been in many fights. So, you are not an innocent. You are a terrorist. Or, perhaps, a soldier?"

Lukas dropped his head back down on the gurney as another piece fell into place. "A warrior. I was, am, a warrior."

The Institution

We know too much to command ourselves very far. Julian Jaynes

DR. JACOBSON LEANED BACK in his sturdy leather chair. It had to be sturdy because he's a large man. An unkind person would say a fat man but he's just a big man once muscled and toned who has gone to seed from the drudgery of a late in life downward career turn. He attempts to wear a face happier than the one that falls over him when he walks out the door and climbs in his car at the end of his shift. He's just arrived and already feels crestfallen. Not a good way to start a bad day.

Driving in this morning, he'd seen a silver-haired man driving a Mercedes sports car. The nice one that holds two golf bags in the trunk. It's the type of car he'd imagined himself driving one day while he was going through med school.

He's supposed to be going through the charts of his first few patients, but he let his mind wander and his heart fill with regret. A part of him knows that his tendency to take this mental path is one of the reasons he's not the great psychiatrist he had every intention of being. He thought of the first wife and the second and dwelt on the fact that alimony could also buy nice cars, but he never achieved that because he made that most terrible of errors that any man with half a brain never really recovers from. He'd married his mistress and therefore created that alimony job opening and the second wife is never as forgiving of a girlfriend as she was when she was that girlfriend.

The air seemed stale to him and he wanted to open a window, but the two in his office are barred and permanently locked. Occasionally he thought of being trapped in this office during a fire. That's on the really bad days.

He tried to focus on the morning report. The girl, Lily, the amnesiac with the smashed head found wandering through her bloody house clutching a knife, had had a nightmare. That night nurse he'd taken to dinner once, Mary-Louise, had given her a sedative at four in the morning. He wished someone would listen to him. No heavy tranquilizers for the patients who already have synaptic glue where there should be memory

30

and cognition. He moved Lily's chart and changed her scheduling so she had a few more hours to come to whatever reality she had left.

Twenty years ago, he would have found Lily a fascinating patient because none of the pieces fit quite right. He would have been poring through textbooks and journals at home with the first wife, sipping good scotch, and trying to find a path into this damaged girl's broken brain. Now he can barely rouse enough curiosity to open his laptop. Besides, he'd made a diagnosis when they brought her in: Transient Global Amnesia brought on by the trauma of killing her family. The hematoma hadn't helped. Except it wasn't living up to the transient part since it was still present. He had to assume the head wound had scrambled things and not being a neurosurgeon, and not having the energy, he wasn't going to delve into that wound nor did he have the budget to pay for that sort of thing.

The amnesia could also just be a dodge to stay off death row. It takes all sorts to fill up an institution.

He didn't capitalize the I, except on formal correspondence.

He missed the old days when someone who killed his or her family like she had would be in the super-max. So much for progress. Except it was exactly the progress he'd lobbied for years ago along with his other more socially conscious colleagues. The difference, now, was that they were on boards and talk shows and publishing books and he's the one dealing with the reality for little pay in this appalling place.

The key to Lily's treatment was accepting that she'd already killed the people she needed to kill for whatever reason the synapses firing in her brain had settled upon at that fateful moment. So, Lily was pretty much a waste of time, except for the stories she sometimes told about her dreams. He'd have found those interesting years ago, but these days, what does it matter? It isn't like she's ever getting out of here.

He flipped open the next chart. A bulimic. Shut it. Next. An anorexic cutter and then two borderlines. All young girls and he wondered again how humans can become so jaded at such a young age. He actually knew the textbook answer, and then he wondered if knowing all the answers about human behavior put him in this rut of career despair.

Twenty years ago, there had still been the thrill of believing the anorexic would eat or the cutter would go to law school and live happily-ever-after. He even once had hoped that the borderlines, with the benefit of his dialectic talk therapy, would see that there could be some emotional stability and that they weren't walking around with a runaway train for a brain and no one at the switches.

But those are the dreams of young doctors in the first flush of residency who haven't quite figured out that they are drawn to the profession because they have their own trains running on rickety tracks to worry about. Sometimes he wanted to look at his patients and say the best way to get yourself a bit squared away is to sit on *this* side of the desk and tell other people how to control themselves. Of course, it didn't always work but it did provide a structure for a mind sorely needing one.

He thought of the day he met Jeannie, his first mistress and second wife.

Now he's going down the rabbit hole and he can't fight it.

He'd been at the height of his enthusiasm for his chosen career and the height of his profession, ensconced in the office his first wife had decorated and with a solidly booked private practice.

He played two rounds of golf every weekend at the country club and joked in the locker room with the other doctors. Surgeons who replaced the same knee day in and day out. OB/GYN's who stared up the same vaginas, thankful he'd chosen a different specialty, especially when he could pick his patients and limit himself to the neurotic and merely depressed. Not deeply depressed because then suicide was an issue. But the housewives who found their lives boring and dull. The anxious non-flyers who chain smoked on their terraces with a bottle of wine but were too terrified to sit on a bridge in their BMWs.

He had weeded out the borderlines who skipped appointments and failed to pay and the narcissists who needed a year of being told they were fabulous before they got bored and walked away. But that day he didn't weed out the beautiful, charming sociopath because even psychiatrists have a difficult time recognizing when they are being played, especially when the player is lovely and incredible skillful.

Now that he was in the deepest part of the rabbit hole, he went over the list he conjures up from time to time that enumerated her traits now so obvious to him but then nothing, nada, a blank, as if all his training had flown out the window when she walked in the door. Or took off on a runaway train taking with it all his sensibilities right at the moment he needed them most.

She had been so charming and, while seductive, he could see her straining to hide that as most beautiful women do when they want to leave that outside the room and be taken seriously as a human and not just a gorgeous woman. Only later, too late, would he realize it was an elaborate act inside an act and she was rather brilliant at it. Sometimes he consoled himself that she would have been a difficult morsel for any man to ignore, but then he always came back to the fact that he hadn't been any man. He was being paid to treat her anxiety. It would be anxiety of course; such an easy thing to feign when feigning is your greatest genetic gift.

That's why, even in this place, with it's fetid air and occasional screams and often mutterings, he still did everything within his limited power to avoid the psychopaths milling about and seemingly oh-so-normal, except for the fact that they aren't human. He now thought of them as a separate species. A snake in human skin. Especially the intelligent ones who can crush a life's work and achievements as easily as the anaconda wraps around a lame deer.

He glanced at the stack of files. Someone like Lily? So obvious when you use a knife, and the wounds as so clear. The ones who don't use a knife are the dangerous ones. The ones who use his own mind against him.

And that's what really bothered him most. That Jeannie had seen his limp so easily and on the very first day. He'd written her a script for Xanax the same hour he'd met her, trying to avoid glancing at the long slim legs crossing and uncrossing as she sat on the couch to the side of his then so sturdy chair, because he hadn't yet turned to hugging food for comfort.

He really should have felt his own limp then because if she'd been a skinny, 15 year old boy, his jeans drooping below non-existent hips and his eyes darkened by lack of sleep and his cuticles chewed bare, he wouldn't have written that script even though that boy did need some relief. He remembered years later finding the bottle of Xanax in her medicine cabinet and they were all still there. Why wouldn't they be? She was a snake; she never felt anxious about a thing. She could lie in the deep grass all day long, quite comfortable just waiting.

He almost didn't hear the knock and was startled when Doctor Jenkins walked in without waiting for permission.

"I could have been in session!" Jacobson protested.

Jenkins wasn't buying it. "Right. I only knocked because I didn't want to walk in on you jerking off to some porn on your computer."

That reminder caused Jacobson to flush beet red and surrender what little outrage he had. "What do you want?"

She walked to his desk and pushed the pile of folders from a neat stack into a spread deck of mental disorders. She leaned over and tapped one. "She's mine. Do an outtake session, sign the paperwork, and then send her up."

Jacobson leaned forward to read the name. Lily Cole. Not surprising. "I didn't make that determination and…"

The look on Jenkins's face took the puff out of his limp sails.

Jenkins stood straight, folding her arms across her chest. Not in the classic subconscious defensive mode, but more of an 'I own you', commanding posture. "How long have you been here?" she asked.

It bothered him that she didn't know; that his arrival hadn't registered on her radar. "Eight months."

"You really are clueless about this place, aren't you?"

Not a question a psychiatrist should ask, since it was bent so negatively. So he didn't reply.

Jenkins smiled, no humor, just coldness. "Still upset about your divorce? Your failed practice?"

Jacobson blinked, not understanding how she could have no idea when he'd arrived at this place, but know those things about him. Given his recent reflections, his defenses kicked in, fearing he had another anaconda in the office, just a different sort in a white coat. Not seductive at all. Sly and cunning and bearing considerable watching.

Jenkins shook her head. "I can't believe you've had her here this long and never moved her upstairs. You're lucky to still be alive."

Now she was demolishing Jacobson's theory that Lily Cole had killed the only people she needed to kill. He steepled his fingers, taking his best professional 'I know what I'm doing' position with his desk between himself and Jenkins. It didn't occur to him to remember how many hours he'd spent practicing that pose and others in front of a mirror so many years ago and that someone like Jenkins could see through it so easily.

"If she's such a threat, I can't believe *you've* left her down here this long. You get the intake file same as I do. Seems like the screw up was on your end."

Jenkins didn't respond.

"Why now?" Jacobson asked, emboldened by her silence.

Jenkins seemed distracted. "They screwed up at trial. It was a slam-dunk. They never delved far enough. Still, she ended up here by protocol, so that's something."

"What are you talking about?" Jacobson asked. "What protocol?"

"She has no one out there," Jenkins said. "No one asking about her. To the world she doesn't exist. No one here does." Jenkins gave him the look that was starting to really get under his skin. The 'you know nothing'. "She was here for months and you never picked up anything?"

"Picked up what?" Jacobson said. "She's suffering from—"

Jenkins cut him off. "I've seen the file. Transient Global Amnesia?" Jenkins leaned forward, putting her fists on the desk and staring at him. "You really think she's run of the mill? Your standard whack job who offed her family in a fugue state? And once she killed them, she won't ever kill again?"

Jacobson could only nod, surprised at her crude terminology.

Jenkins gave a shake of her head. "You think you work for the state? How much do they pay you? Sixty grand? You used to clear that in a month or two in private practice didn't you?"

Jacobson narrowed his eyes. Jenkins *was* rattled. Too aggressive, too talkative, too everything. "So you're a few pay grades above me."

Jenkins laughed. "We don't work for the state. And the Fourth Floor? We're—" she stopped. "Just get her upstairs. Today."

Jenkins left as abruptly as she'd entered.

Jacobson waited two minutes, he timed it on his watch, and before making the call to have Lily Cole brought to his office. The mini-protest made him feel slightly better.

The knock came after a few minutes.

"Enter," Jacobson called out in his best command, 'I am in charge' voice.

Lily Cole walked right in and sat so confidently, so calmly, and didn't appear to be bothered by the aftereffects of the sedative. Jacobson was gratified to see her like this, because it meant she really was a snake. He listened to her ramble on about some dream and waking here and there and imagined her holding that knife and smiling and then calmly changing her face into a mask of terrified confusion as the police entered that house. He pretended to take notes, but he accepted she was another snake and everything she said was a lie and that she wasn't going to be his problem any more. She could go join all the other snakes, non-inmates included, up on the Fourth Floor.

He was almost pleased with himself because really, who did she think she was? Fool me once Jeannie, but Lily, I'm onto you. He leaned back farther into the leather ignoring the shriek of the springs which were fighting hard to keep up. As Lily droned on, he remembered the day before Jeannie had first walked into his office when he'd shot a 78 and what a lovely day that had been.

He glanced at the clock on his desk, then wondered why he cared if he'd given Lily Cole enough time. Old habit. He was feeling pretty good that he'd gotten the last word with Jenkins and now he was getting rid of this patient. The day was on the upswing.

He'd rattled Jenkins. She'd come to him, which meant that somehow, he had some hand. He frowned, replaying the conversation with Jenkins in his head, wondering how much he actually didn't know? *Did* he have hand?

"I'm sorry," Lily Cole said. "Did I say something wrong?"

Jacobson peered at her. If it wasn't Transient Global Amnesia, and he'd already known he was wrong, he didn't need that blowhole Jenkins to tell him that, what was with this girl? Just a psychopath who got triggered?

"No, nothing," Jacobson said, giving that vague wave for her to continue to ramble on which all shrinks master very early in the careers. A nonverbal re-assurance that he could do in his sleep.

She was blathering now about some house in the woods and flowers.

Does any of this really matter? Jacobson wondered. Lily Cole was heading to the Fourth Floor and she was Jenkins's problem.

"Very good," he said, cutting her off in mid-confused-sentence. "That's it for today." *And forever*, he thought.

The girl blinked. A line appeared in her forehead as she frowned.

Jacobson hit the correct little button underneath his desk, summoning the orderly, because he wasn't in the mood to deal with any lip, not when she was now Jenkins's property.

The door swung open and Mike came in.

The girl got to her feet, well trained in the way of the Institution, resigned. But the line was still there in her forehead.

"Be careful," she suddenly said, apropos of nothing he could discern.

"Excuse me?" Jacobson said. He glanced past her at Mike, who shrugged, used to crazy.

"You're not a bad man, Doctor Jacobson," the girl said. "Be careful."

And then she was gone. Jacobson scrawled his signature on the transfer order to the Fourth Floor. In the months he'd been here, he'd sent a dozen or so up to Jenkins and the Fourth Floor, but no one had ever come back down.

He'd never though much of it, but his upswing had hit Lily's warning, like a softball into a bat and his hand over Jenkins faded to holding not much of anything except a very strange situation.

Snakes everywhere. He thought of Jeannie living with her new boyfriend, no thought of getting married and stopping the alimony. Jenkins doing whatever it is Jenkins did up there on the Fourth Floor. Working for whomever she worked for. Lily butchering her little brother and sister.

Jacobson took Lily's file, the transfer order on top, slid it inside a new folder with no label, and left his office. He went to the small room that held the single copy machine that served this part of the Institution. He carefully unclipped Lily's file, put it upside down in the feeder, and then hit the copy button.

The machine went to work, sucking it in, page by page, whirring.

It came to an abrupt halt two-thirds of the way through. Muttering curses, Jacobson opened up the machine.

No one ever filled up the paper like they were supposed to.

He loaded, and then hit copy again and the machine went back to work. When it was done, Jacobson took the originals, thumped them so that the two holes on top lined up, and put them back in the clip, folding the prongs down. He took the copy and stuffed that into the new folder. He took Lily's file to the nurse's desk, dropped it off with the transfer order, then headed back to his office to put the copy in his small safe.

One could never be too careful with all these snakes around.

Then he remembered something. He went to the copying room, opened the machine, pulled the remaining blank paper out and left the machine empty.

* * *

Lara walked into the commons room more disconcerted than ever and that was saying a lot for her in this place. She had stared at Dr. Jacobson because she didn't remember him, although his office was the same as Dr. Jenkins. Except Jenkins hadn't been so fat that her chair was nearly exploding from the pressure. He had looked back at her with an odd familiarity as if he knew her only too well, so it made sense for her to accept this new doctor and just add Dr. Jenkins into the very long list now of things sorta remembered, forgotten, not real, or just plain lost.

She had no idea why she'd said that last thing about being careful or him not being a bad man. It had just occurred to her. Fit with everything else she had no idea about.

The oatmeal sat in her stomach, refusing to budge and she felt a bit sick, but she trudged into the open area of the ward, which someone with no sense of humor had painted a sickly green that gave all the women sitting around an even more sallow look than women who rarely went out of doors should have. They were allowed time outside in the courtyard but it was winter out there with naked trees and freezing benches that felt like frozen steel tearing through your jeans. Funny that it had been so much warmer when she escaped because she no longer thought of it as a long, complicated dream within this nightmare of knowing nothing and understanding even less than that. It was a memory of an escape and she clung to it and savored it for the hints it might contain about her past. She'd kept going over the things she knew in the dream—the sheets, the gluten free bread, but Dr. Jacobson hadn't seemed interested. He'd stared at her blankly, seeming to find nothing enthralling about it all and she'd felt her last bit of hope disappear.

Lara sat next to a woman who cradled a stuffed cat missing one glass eye as she stroked and stroked its nearly stroked-off fake fur. She wondered if the woman had brought that with her or found it in the bin of other worn stuffed animals, and boxed games all missing pieces, and packs of cards, four of which still wouldn't make a full deck. It seemed to Lara to be a horribly frustrating place for people all bound in their own layers of personal frustration. It seemed like a leaky rubber life raft in the middle of the ocean full of terrified non-swimmers with a stern nurse standing aft and asking everyone *is there a problem* with no guile at all.

So, she knew boats, but at this rate of remembering she'd get her old life back right around the time they'd have to move her to the geriatric ward and spoon feed her applesauce while she stared out the window and tried to recall what the squirrels were called because her youthful amnesia would have just slid into dementia.

Lara tugged at the bottom of her shirt, imagining it down to her knees, when Mike walked up, looking not bored or stoic as usual, but concerned, she realized that that was his most terrifying face—genuine concern.

"Why'd you say that to Doctor Jacobson?" he asked.

"I don't know."

Mike shook his head.

"What?" Lara asked. "What's wrong?"

"We're moving you kid. Dr. Jacobson's orders."

"Moving me to where?"

"Another part."

"But why?" she asked. "Just 'cause I said that?"

He shook his head again. "I don't think so. But it didn't help." He held up a clipboard. "I just read 'em kid. I don't explain them. Come on, it's not so bad. I hear the food's better."

Really? Lara thought. The same horrible industrial kitchen had some corner area where they made the good stuff?

"Let's get your stuff," Mike said.

But then she realized something. The rumors. "Where am I going?"

"To get your stuff," Mike avoided.

"Where am I being moved to?"

Mike shook his head. "Let's get your stuff, kid."

They went to her room. It didn't take long. Everything she had fit into the single black garbage bag that Mike handed her. As she stuffed those stupid jeans into it, she heard something crinkle, but with him hovering over her shoulder, she didn't dare check to see what it was.

Lara followed as Mike led her down the hall, unlocked and locked a few gates, and then she saw a man who looked nothing like Mike, although he was wearing the same uniform. He had one face—scary—and it was so creased onto him that she knew it never moved toward a smile or even a frown. It was the face of a man so pissed off by life and the human condition that he didn't notice a young girl with perky breasts, a flat stomach, and a not-perfect butt, as she now knew, but certainly one above average. He looked through her like he was a busy man with a briefcase sidestepping a legless man wearing a moth-eaten skullcap.

He took the clipboard from Mike and reached for her wrist in a way that surprised her and she instinctively pulled back.

He said in a voice so harsh that she withdrew another step. "You wanna do it easy or hard? It doesn't matter to me."

No kidding, Lara thought. *The second coming wouldn't matter to you.*

"Easy, Sam," Mike said. "She's a good kid."

Sam read a bit of the clipboard. "Good kid? Are you getting soft? How'd she end up staying down here this long? We should have had her since June. Jenkins is pissed."

Lara started to turn and tried to run away, not from Sam so much, but at the idea that she'd been here since June. Mike gently laced his fingers around her arm, holding her still.

The horribly gnarled bare limbs outside the barred windows had been full of green leaves dancing in warm sunshine when she got to this place was such a terrible and frightening thought. She wanted to run back to the commons room and climb into that woman's lap, tossing away the worn cat, and be stroked on the back over and over, while being told that it would be OK. But nothing was OK. Even the little she'd thought was OK was wretched, because suddenly for the first time in this looney bin house of horrors with no clue *who* she was, she knew *what* she was: she was insane. Crazy, lalaland nuts. She didn't feel crazy; she felt lost and alone in a world that came back to her a word and an image at a time but until now she'd never thought she was just plain nuts. She began to cry hysterically and dug her feet in as hard as smooth shiny linoleum would allow her very cheap slippers, which wasn't much.

"Kid, don't," Mike said. "You're OK. It's going to be OK."

But he wasn't stroking her back, he was pushing her into the arms of the man who was sick and tired of her before he ever saw her because she was just another loon in a day filled with crazy, crazier, and craziest.

But then Sam bent down to her ear and whispered so only she could hear, "do you want to do it hard because I prefer that."

And while no part of his face moved, Lara saw a new glint in his eye that told her he still did have small pleasures left to him and he'd be happy to turn her into one of them. She knew, just knew, that edging wouldn't work with him.

She forced her body to be still and said in the calmest voice she could muster, "I'm going to be good. I'm sorry. I just got scared."

Sam nodded at Mike. "She's smart. Why are they all so smart?"

Lara wanted to ask who *they* were, but she was determined to make it wherever she was going without seeing that glint in Sam's eyes again.

39

Actually ever again would be better and from now on whatever the best behavior was, Lara was determined to do even better because this was her life right now in this minute and every minute which would follow because did it really matter who you were when you were bat shit crazy. She highly doubted it, and she somehow knew something very real about herself in this hallway and that was that she did not like being hurt. Lara assumed most people didn't want to be hurt, but she felt the first real hard truth she'd known since she was actually aware that she was here and not someplace else. She had a deep and abiding fear of being hurt. She stood straight and stared straight ahead unsure of where she was going, but very sure that she wanted to get there with as little fuss as possible. Sam was a man who'd split a lip as easily as he'd pick the string from a green bean or clean his teeth with a matchbook cover. She hadn't even seen a matchbook in her real time here. She was already thinking of it that way: her real time

She looked back at Mike with enough pleading that she knew he'd give her something back: "What's the date?"

"December third."

What have I been doing for all these months?

Mike gave her a bit of a wink and a forced smile. "You'll be OK, kid."

And her face flushed hot for a second because she could now see plainly in his tight smile a bit of what she'd been doing.

"You gonna be a good girl?" Sam asked.

Lara whispered, "yes, I am," and stopped herself from saying *Sam-I-Am, Yes-I-Am*.

He took her through another set of locked gates and into a lobby area, but without the plants and nice carpets.

What plants and nice carpets she wondered? When had she passed through here before?

He led her to an elevator but there was no up or down button, just a scanner. He waved his ID card at the device and the doors slid open. He ushered her in and as she feared, pushed the top button: FOUR. As the doors shut them inside the small space, Lara began to wonder if she was claustrophobic. Sam-I-Am wouldn't understand and use it as a reason to grapple her to the floor and do other things she tried not to think about.

Then he began to whistle. She knew the tune but his mouth didn't move enough for it to be natural, so he was doing it for her. *To unnerve her*, she thought, and she stared up at the ceiling and pretended to be somewhere else. But there were so few places available in her head, so she imaged Martha's perfect garage, the soothing emptiness of it, and how it had made all their voices echo, all their voices being the three of them, her and Martha and Jake, but when you have so few people up there three is enough.

It was a slow elevator and when it jarred, she thought they were there but it was only the second floor. He kept whistling the same few notes over and over and by the time the doors finally slid open to the fourth floor she recognized it but couldn't remember the title—'*I shot a Man in Reno just to watch him die*'.

When he sensed she got it, he stopped as abruptly as he'd started whistling and if he was expecting some response from her he failed to get it and not because it wasn't there but Lara was more interested in the fact that she did seem to know Johnny Cash.

He led her down a darker hallway, the floors weren't so highly polished, and the lights were either dimmer from neglect or some reasoning she didn't want to think about. The gates were made of sturdier stuff, bars instead of metal grates. Lara knew this was less a place to keep people from idly wandering about, but rather to keep them tightly locked in, as in keeping the girl who killed her family away from the rest of the nice people.

A small foyer beckoned, with a solid looking door on the other side. Another device that Sam-I-Am waved his ID at. The door hissed open on some hidden arm and Lara knew it was a thick door, a very thick one.

Why did they need such a thick door?

Sam-I-Am pushed her through with more force necessary considering how very good she'd been. They walked down a length of corridor with more thick doors on either side with small windows made for peeping inside and she knew this was the prison part of the Institution.

It was now time to capitalize the I.

Lara had not made a good impression on Dr. Jacobson and she had no idea why. Maybe it was something from all the other months she didn't remember or maybe they'd found real evidence that she had killed her family besides a bloody shirt? If they had, she wished they'd show it to her. She could live here forever knowing she wasn't just insane but an insane murderer. Lara had finally reached the point where she'd believe anything about herself as long as it was something to believe in. Even something horrible, because this feeling of floating along on a stream of nothing, knowing nothing, was becoming unbearable.

At the end of the corridor was a glassed-in nurse's station, or guard station, or whatever you wanted to call it. Sam-I-Am waited as a guard dressed in black, with an actual gun in a holster, which scared Lara, looked at Sam-I-Am's proffered ID card, and then indicated a tray he slid open.

Sam-I-Am dropped Lara's file into the tray. The man pulled the tray back, opened the file, read the contents, checked a computer screen off to the side, looked at Lara once more as if not sure she was the girl whose name was on the file, and then he nodded.

The door buzzed open.

A woman in a white coat was waiting on the other side.

"Hello, Lily," the woman said with genuine warmth in her voice. "I'm Doctor—"

"Jenkins." As soon as she said it, Lara knew that was a mistake on several levels.

Jenkins smiled hardened for a moment. "We've never met."

Lara nodded her head toward the name stitched on the white coat, scrambling back from her faux paus. "I'm sorry, doctor," she said, trying to stay on an even keel in a thunderstorm.

She could feel Sam-I-Am's glare and knew she'd pay for speaking out of turn.

Doctor Jenkins stared back, unblinking, and then she seemed to let it slide. "You're just in time for lunch. I'll show you the cafeteria." She waved a hand at Sam-I-Am, dismissing him, which Lara thought wasn't very perceptive of someone who was supposed to be trained on the human psyche. But Lara also sensed Jenkins didn't like Sam-I-Am much either and that made Lara like her a little.

"So, here on the fourth floor, we all eat together?" Lara wondered aloud because on the not-fourth-floor they ate in their rooms and hung around stroking stuffed animals together for the little time they were allowed out. But here it looked like they ate together and then hung out in their rooms stroking God knows what.

"Eating issues are a concern downstairs with some patients," Dr. Jenkins said. "Not here."

Oh, that makes sense, Lara thought. Here we just kill people, downstairs are all the folks who'd rather kill themselves than eat a French fry. There were probably people here who killed people and then ate them, which she oddly thought made them a tad saner than those starving themselves to death downstairs despite getting paid to eat.

Wherever Lara had been the last months, she very much wanted to return right now.

Dr. Jenkins unlocked another door and Lara smelled coffee. Good coffee and the low murmurings of excited voices talking about crazy things.

Dr. Jenkins showed her where to get a tray and took her through the line, encouraging her to try the soup, it was good, and then took her to a table where a man and woman sat.

Jenkins said, "Jim this is Lily and Lily this is Maria. I'll see you later."

And with that, she was gone with the same clicking of low heels that Lara had heard just the night before. Or was it a night? Was it a six months? Maybe her whole life she'd just been in this place shuffled from floor to floor by sadistically inclined guards who whistled Johnny Cash tunes.

Sam-I-Am leaned close and whispered, so only she could hear, "welcome to the Fourth Floor. You're mine now."

Black Site, The Negev Desert, Israel

"The Trojan War was directed by hallucinations. And the soldiers who were so directed were not at all like us. They were noble automatons who knew not what they did." Julian Jaynes

"'A WARRIOR'?" RAHEL didn't seem impressed. "You surrendered so easily. So afraid to die."

"Not afraid to die. Afraid of killing others." Lukas's stared straight up, at the bright light, but he didn't seem affected by it.

"Even worse for a warrior," Rahel said. "A warrior's only purpose is to kill enemies."

Lukas blinked, turned his head toward her. "Really? I don't know."

"Who did you serve, warrior?"

There was no derision in the term.

"I don't know." He shook his head. "I don't remember being a warrior. I'm just really hungry."

"Stop with the food," she said. "We got the others in your cell. Every one of them. No one cares about you. You have no family or friends asking about you. That's very bad for you."

"Worse than this?" Lukas asked, indicating the gurney he was strapped to with a tilt of his jaw.

Rahel glanced at the camera, then back at him. "If you have no connections out in the world who care about you, then you can disappear...completely disappear...and no one will be the wiser."

That triggered something from the before and he shivered.

Rahel noted the reaction. "What is it?"

"Someone *is* coming."

"Here? Who?"

"'*My name is legion*'," Lukas whispered.

Rahel cocked her head for a moment. "'*For we are many*'," she finally said. "Mark. Five Nine. I know both books. Old and new. Quoting scripture won't—"

Lukas shook his head. "It is not from a book. Old or new. It is from a man. A dangerous man."

"From your group in the cellar?" She indicated the dark television. "From him? He's no longer dangerous."

"No." Lukas closed his eyes. "I can hear him say it but I don't see see him. Then—" Lukas cried out in pain.

Rahel got up and walked over to him. She reached down, took his chin in her gloved hand and forced his head toward. "Look at me. Then what? Who said it?"

Lukas opened his eyes. "Death. Legion is death. And he is coming."

LARA

"The unlocatable location of things thought about." Julian Jaynes

I SIT DOWN NEXT TO JIM AND MARIA, whom I'd already been introduced to as Jake and Martha on an estate on the other side of Portland. It sorta feels like I'm on a short bus with about five people and we just keep turning a corner. It's all right turns and ending up back in the same places. I wonder if they remember me as clearly as I remember them, but watching Maria eat a hotdog in four bites, bun and all, robs me of that hope cause this chick here only looks like Martha. And Jim has the appearance of a man whose garage is stuffed to the rafters with three broken lawnmowers, rusty old tools, and maybe a barrel with a dead girl in it.

Jim-not-Jake smiles that Jake-from-the-truck-leer. "You got a nice ass."

When in Rome. "Well, thanks for noticing, Jim." I add a big toothy grin cause crazy is as crazy does. No one else is even looking my way and there are about thirty people clustered about, stuffing their faces and Mike was right, the food is better, go figure.

Maria still has a piece of bun going when she says, "That's rude. Don't talk like that to her. She's just a kid."

Cripes, I think, how old you gotta be in this place to not be a kid anymore? I have a sickening feeling that I'm going to find out.

"Shit, Maria, a kid? Sam told me that she murdered her whole family."

Maria draws a startled breath and begins to choke on that bit of bun and I wonder if I know how to do the Heimlich and figure I probably do since I know its name.

But she gags it down and says, "Really? You killed them all?"

All? Interesting question I hadn't considered before. I was told four but I'm actually not sure how many there were, but I should keep the official story going here. "Yes." I take a sip of soup and don't slurp a drop. My, I do have some fine manners. I wonder where I learned them.

"Whatcha in for, Jim?" I ask cause it occurs to me that we're all criminally insane here and not just wackos lying around all day long. I instinctively know you survive here by fessing up and staying fessed up.

"I cut up a college student and kept her in a footlocker."

Well, I was close for a guess. "Only one college student?" I grin again, comrade in crazy.

"They only found one," he says and doesn't smile at all, just stares off into space with the creepy look of a guy remembering some rather gross fun times.

"How did *you* do it?" Maria asks me with all the nonchalance of *how did you make these great cookies—is this real butter?*

"I used a knife," I say and go back to my soup.

Maria shivers a bit. "Oh, that's so hard."

She sounds as if she knows of what she speaks.

"Is it? I don't remember."

"Won't work," Jim says, confusing me for a second. "Everyone tries that 'I don't remember thing'. Jenkins don't care."

Maria takes a sip of diet coke and says, "I shot my husband. Much easier, not so personal and it's so hard to kill someone with a knife. I looked it up."

"Why'd you shoot him Maria? Just to watch him die?" I ask.

"Oh, no," she says. "He beat me."

"That sounds reasonable," I say. "I'm surprised a good lawyer couldn't turn that into self-defense."

Jim laughs. "He beat her at gin rummy."

"He cheated," she says, using a tone that implies she had all the reason in the world.

Jim starts to crack his knuckles, all ten of them individually. I put down my spoon, imagining how it sounds like college girls' bones cracking. Yeah, I can pretend to be tough in here to survive, but I don't think that I belong here.

He's on his third knuckle when he says, "And he cheated on you too, Maria. That's why I think you did it."

"Was not," she says. "I shot him right over the card table in the living room. His face fell into the cards."

"Was he holding aces and eights?" I say.

"What?" Maria is puzzled.

And I think two things: how do I know that and what a boring lifetime this is going to be. I glance around the room hoping to see perhaps a cannibal to have dinner with. They all look like normal people talking about the weirdest things ever and then I see the truck driver—the one who tried to fuck me in my sleep, which I think is rather odd; among a whole shitload of odd. I stand up and say my excuses to them but they don't notice me much because they're lost in an obviously long ongoing debate on exactly which cheating caused Maria to blow her husband's head off.

Does it really matter?

I walk over and sit across from him and can tell right away that he has never seen me before. I feel a bit sad over that; like somehow I hadn't mattered, enough to be remembered at all even in while being raped in a dream. He's sitting next to a boy close to my age. Well, I guess I am a kid cause I don't think of him as a man but he is a cute boy, with longish hair that curls in tendrils and gives his smooth perfect skin a rather angelic quality. He looks at me with the brownest eyes with the longest lashes I've ever seen. Course I don't remember how many deep brown eyes with long lashes I've seen so maybe I shouldn't say longest because that's a superlative. Now how do I know that? *Good with grammar, knows Wild Bill fatal hand, and Johnny Cash tunes.* What does that add up to?

The boy says, "Hello, Lily. It's good to see you again."

Of all the crap I've gone through today, his knowing me is the most shocking. I lean over and whisper, "Where do you know me from?" is a big secret in this room instead of college girls in footlockers. It's so very odd to be looking at a complete stranger who knows me when the man sitting next to him had tried to put his dick in me and doesn't know me from Adam.

"I'm Seth," the boy says, his lashes batting a few times. "We went to high school together."

"Really?" I'm interested now. "Where?"

"George Washington."

My heart sinks. Wichita. Really? The hits keep on coming.

I try to keep the brave face. "What was I like? Did I do great in English?"

He gives me an odd look. "You weren't there long. About six months. Your family moved around a lot I heard. Sam said you killed them."

Geez, Sam-I-Am must live on the grapevine.

Seth turns to truck driver and nods. "This is Claude."

Claude? Really, what are you 35? Who names a kid Claude in this century? I hope you killed those parents. I just nod my greeting, because something about Claude bothers me. He doesn't even look up from his soup when Seth introduces us, so my nod is lost.

Seth says, "Lily, did you kill them? I never saw that in you."

"Thank you dude, but seems I did. With a knife, a big knife, so let's not get into how hard that was because I don't remember."

Seth says, "I don't think you do remember. Maybe you didn't kill them?"

"Maybe I didn't, but it's my story in here," and I wave my hand about, "and I'm sticking to it."

Seth says, "Yeah, probably a good idea."

Claude looks up from his soup, which he's eating all wrong. "You know where that came from—my story and I'm sticking to it?"

"No, not a clue, don't even know how I know it."

He puts his spoon down for which I was grateful and steeples his hands under his chin like a professor getting ready to discuss the Peloponnesian wars--*yeah, no clue.* And he says, "There was this guy out drinking and fucking some broad—"

Yeah, I think, just like the Peloponnesian wars.

"—and he's banging her and loses all track of time and he's drunk and knows he needs to get home before his wife wakes up. So, he rushes home as the sun is coming up and climbs into bed with her and pretends to wake up."

Yeah, gross I think.

"And she says, '*where were you all night?*' And he says, '*out playing poker*'."

Luckily not with Maria I think.

Claude was pushing on through the story in a monotone, as if he had it memorized and told it often. "And the guy says, '*I had a couple of drinks and it was about midnight. I didn't want to wake you up so I slept in the hammock. I just came in a few minutes ago to grab and some real rest cause that hammock ain't the greatest place to sleep. I figured it was late enough now to wake you up.*' And he gives her a bit of cuddle to say OK. We're good here. And she says, '*it's November asshole, I put the hammock in a box in the garage two months ago.*' And he says, '*well that's my story and I'm sticking to it.*'"

I can't help it; I start to laugh and it feels good like I haven't laughed in a long time or not since I can remember. Even Seth laughs and for a moment it all feels normal if normal is a room full of murdering nuts. But laughs can only last so long.

"Why are you in here Seth?" I can't help myself. I just need to know.

"I killed my girlfriend."

Good thing I can't remember anything of old George Washington High or his girlfriend, but it seems like it was a bad place if it produced the two of us. Feeling the vibe still coming off Claude I rattle words out, going for a stab in the dark and I mean no pun here, "Were you drunk?"

Seth shakes his head, his lovely hair swaying around him as if there were a soft fan, and he is in tight jeans and no shirt and a bit of the Calvin sticking out as some photographer said, '*look this way, look that way, look like you murdered your girlfriend.*'

Seth takes a bite of lasagna; the food was way, way better here. He sorta mouths around it, "No, not drunk. Beat her to death with a hammer."

Claude is just watching me now, his soup cooling.

"Was she cheating on you?" I ask. "With another guy or maybe at cards?"

"No, she wanted to break up with me." And he finishes chewing.

It seems almost impolite to not ask Claude what brought him here aside from the unfortunate name.

He starts chuckling. "I shot my neighbor's dog because he wouldn't stop barking."

What the fuck? He shot a dog? I hate to admit how horrified I am because what does that say about all of us that of all I've heard so far, that gets to me? "What kind of dog?"

"A beagle. You know how they have that horrible bark? Sounds like a bay and a bark at the same time? And I worked the night shift and fuck me, but you can only try to sleep through that a few days before you have to blow that sucker away."

"Where did you work?"

"I was an orderly in a nursing home."

And that makes sense. "Did you smother them in their sleep?"

"I like you kid." He grins. "Yeah, a few. You're the only person who's ever asked me that without having seen my file."

Seth puts down his fork. "Hey, Lily. You wanna go fuck behind the dishwasher? There's a spot there that's good and Sam stays away cause I give him all my cigarette rations."

I stand up, but my legs are weak. "That sounds lovely, Seth. Maybe another time. I've had a long and confusing day so I think I'll go lie down for a while."

Claude looks up with a dribble of soup hanging on his lower lip. "Well, be careful cause Sam will get you in your sleep and he won't give you any break till he's tasted that." And Claude seems like he actually cares.

I rush out of there as fast as my legs can carry me.

The room is more like my cell four floors down and the bed is a wafer of foam rubber on a slab of concrete, but I've never wanted to sleep as much as I do at this moment. If Sam shows up I'll just deal but now pulling up the thick woolen blanket I think how odd, this whole blanket thing, and I fall asleep because even a dream is better than these people and this place.

Of course, I'm wrong.

* * *

I'm in a forest but there are paths. Clearly marked paths and I feel as though I know where I am. The trees are half covered in moss, and ferns are growing wild everywhere. It's beautiful and I seem to know where I'm going so I just keep walking, but I'm in no rush. It might be a dream but it's the best place I've been that I can remember, ever, ever. There are even birds flitting by and squirrels and sunlight and it's perfect, perfect.

I keep walking, knowing I'm dreaming, but it's warm with a slight breeze and the outside smells so good and crisp and clean and I really feel like I know where I'm going for once and it's not any place bad and there's no blood.

I come to a fork left or right, and my heart starts pounding because I know this is important, really important, but each way looks pretty much the same. Level, through the thick forest, equally travelled.

So much for that less traveled option.

I decide not to decide, which seems really smart, ha!

Except the dream is in my brain somewhere and it's smarter than me and I hear a loud noise behind me. I look back and the sky is black and the noise is thunder and there's a storm coming and I have to make a choice and keep moving forward, left or right or should I try cutting through the trees, but really, a choice should mean one is good and one is bad, right?

Fifty-fifty, easy peasy.

The woods, beautiful though they are, are so thick with undergrowth and ferns and brambles and blackberries that I know I'll get stuck and then the storm will get me and I'll get worse than wet.

Much worse. Don't know how I know that, except I know dreams and how easy they become nightmares, so I just turn to the left and follow that path, moving a bit faster, even though it's still so beautiful, but there is thunder behind, seeming to just be waiting now.

It turns into a winding trail along the edge of a hill and part way up I come to the largest rock I've ever seen. It's not Ayer's Rock, don't know how I know about that, but it's a big rock and perfectly formed and there is a path all around the outer rim of it and it takes me five minutes to walk all the way around. But, it's a dream; maybe it took me four day or four minutes. The storm seems to approve, staying in the distance, grumbling with thunder and dark sky, but I'm still in the sun.

So maybe I made the right choice?

But, I walk all around the rock again and I hear the lowest sort of sound emitting from it. Not even a sound when I focus, but a dull throb of a noise like when you go swimming and your ears fill with water and you jump up and down on one leg, head bent, till you feel the little trickle of relief. And then start hopping on the other leg.

Except the throb doesn't go away, even though I do try jumping, because who knows, maybe I missed the part of the dream where I was in water, even though my clothes are dry, and I notice they're the same ones from after I had escaped, but not escaped, which, well it's a dream, I gotta go with it.

But then I'm lost. The rock is gone even though I was going round it and there are just paths going every which way and I don't know which to take because I don't know where I'm going and I'm lost. I'm so lost.

The thunder is coming closer, but I hear something else, maybe wind, maybe a car? I leave the trail I'm on and cut through the forest. It doesn't seem as thick as it did before, although the ground is covered in thick moss and I'm running, not sure where my feet are landing. I do think I will break a foot but that seems so small a thing in a dream when waking up is going to be such a nightmare. And really, how much can a broken foot hurt in a dream?

A lot. My foot catches a root and twists so hard and I lean over and throw up some soup, but that was from the Fourth Floor. I limp through the rest of the trees just aiming for the cars I can clearly hear now. I'm limping and staggering and finally I'm on the edge of a two-lane road and the cars aren't many, but they're going by fast as if everyone is in a rush to get wherever it is they know they need to get to, which makes them luckier than me. Finally while I stand there on one foot waving, one does stop.

The driver nods for me to get in but her whole car is full of boxes, the passenger seat is full of boxes and she says, *Hi. I've got a load of jewelry for some stores in town and I'm sorry but if you can fit it I can take you that far. Looks like a storm is coming.*

I'd have tried to fit myself into a rabbit hutch to get off that foot. I'm wedged in, holding a few boxes and I realize the driver is Dr. Jenkins. She, of course, doesn't know me, and I don't even care cause my ankle hurts so bad. Come on, it's a fucking dream. How can you dream pain like this? *It's stupid,* I tell myself.

Jenkins drives about a mile or two and slows down for a curve and I see a drive and a gate. A beautiful gate that I know I've dreamt before and now it's going by and I say, *Please let me out here—I have friends here*

Jenkins says, *That's great, darling.* She nods to my foot and says, *That puppy is gonna hurt when you take off that hiking boot,* and I look down and I am wearing hiking boots. Rather smart of me in a dream, since it seems I upgraded my foot apparel from my escape, not escape. I hobble out of the car, trying to leave the boxes as neat as when I found them. I'm in front of the gate and there's a pole with a speaker box. It reminds me of those clunky boxes you hang on the side of your car for sound at a drive in movie. I feel bad because I realize a place like Wichita, Kansas, probably still has drive-in theaters and someone who'd iron that horrible shirt would take the family to a movie in a car.

I push call on the box. My heart sinks as I hear a voice I don't recognize say *Hello, may I help you?*

And I say, *Yes I'm looking for Martha.*

And the woman says, *Oh, she's in her office let me get her.*

And I almost collapse with relief. My ankle is killing me and I lean against the pole and I hear Martha's voice, it is her voice, and I can't help myself, I begin to cry and she says, *Who is this?*

And I say, *Lily.*

She says, *Lily? The Lily I found and brought here?*

Yes, that Lily. How many Lily's does she know, I wonder for a second?

What happened to you? Where did you go?

I'm close to fainting now and I ask, *Martha, what happened to me?*

And she says, *How would I know? Jake and I put you to bed and the next morning you were just gone. You did make the bed though, so that was nice, even though you didn't need to because I had to wash the sheets anyway. You should have just stripped it and piled the sheets.*

Martha, I'm hurt please let me in.

Okay. I'll send Jake with the truck to get you but I don't really understand how you can leave in the middle of the night and show back up a year later like nothing is going on.

I gasp. *A year?*

Yeah," she says and the gate slides open and it sounds like the humming from the rock.

And Jenkins, seeing it open, drives off.

Black Site, The Negev Desert

"If we would understand the Scientific Revolution correctly, we should always remember that its most powerful impetus was the unremitting search for hidden divinity. As such, it is a direct descendant of the breakdown of the bicameral mind." Julian Jaynes

RAHEL LET GO OF LUKAS'S CHIN. "You need to explain. What do you mean? Who is coming?"

A single tear trickled out of Lukas's left eye and slid down the side of his face to drop into the cheap sheet the gurney was covered with. "I am a warrior. It is my duty to protect her. But I am here. Trapped."

The door to the room protested open and Rahel hurried out of his sight. There was a harsh argument in Hebrew, Rahel and a man, and then she was back, the door squeaking shut.

"My associates are getting impatient. They think you are playing me. They believe I have lost control of the interrogation. That you are acting crazy. We've seen it before. "

Lukas looked at her. "Acting crazy or really crazy?"

Rahel shrugged. "Does it matter?"

"A great deal. You need to let me go. I have to go to her. It is my duty to protect her. The wounds you see on my body, I sustained those protecting her."

"You're just a boy," Rahel said, without much conviction because the scars backed up part of his story. "I cannot let you go."

He nodded toward her. "Your name. Rahel. What does it mean?"

She blinked at the abrupt shift. "It's a form of Rachel. Sometimes I wish my parents had spelled—"

"You are not telling the truth."

Rahel sighed. She reached up and removed the balaclava. The left side of her face was rippled with scar tissue. "Lamb. It means lamb."

"But you are no lamb," Lukas said. "Why did you come here? Did you think it would salve the pain?"

Rahel began unfastening the straps. When she was done, she reached underneath the gurney and grabbed a stained white coverall and tossed it to him. "Put that on."

"Are you letting me go?"

"I need answers," Rahel said. "Now. Or else I leave this room and my associate enters. He will not be gentle. He will not be patient. You might believe me a lamb, then he is a lion. You are no longer tied up. If you are a warrior, then we are equals now. Speak to me as an equal. Focus on my questions and answer them as I ask them. Do you understand?"

Lukas tugged on the coverall, buttoning it. "Yes." He sat on the edge of the gurney.

"You say someone is coming. Who?"

"Legion. He is Legion. That is their name."

"That doesn't make sense. That's from the Bible. Mark, Chapter Five, verses one thru thirteen."

Lukas pointed at the earpiece that had been hidden under the balaclava. "Is that what they are telling you?"

Rahel plowed on. "It refers to demons that Jesus exorcises. In a place called Gerasenes. Or Jerash, which is now in Jordan. Are you from Jordan?"

"Is that your question or one fed to you?"

"Your time is running out."

"I don't know where I am from," Lukas said. "I know I must protect her."

"Who is her?"

Lukas frowned. "I can't quite remember. She is there, on the edge of my mind, so important, but I can't reach her."

"You are to protect her from this Legion person?"

"They are Legion," Lukas said. "But yes, each of them is also Legion."

"Demons?" There was no tone to the question, as if she were willing to accept an answer either way.

"Killers," Lukas said. "They deal in death. They live to kill. To them it is everything. Their very essence. If they cannot kill, they have nothing."

"Where are these killers from?" Rahel asked.

Lukas stiffened. "They are from the darkness."

"Clarify," Rahel snapped.

"That is all I know right now."

"You say this killer is coming. For this person or for you?"

"I don't know." Lukas looked at her. "I think he's coming here. I can't tell you how I know that. I just feel it."

"Then you are safe. This is one of the most secure places in Israel."

"Not from death. No one is secure from death."

"If this killer is after her, why would he come here?" Rahel asked.

"I don't know." Lukas stood up. "You must let me go."

"And where would you go?" Rahel asked.

"To her."

"You don't know who this person is you are supposed to protect," Rahel pointed out. "All you know of the threat is that it is someone called Legion who you believe is the personification of death. Yet, earlier, when I asked, you said the Fates controlled death."

Lukas put his hands to his temples and pressed, as if squeezing knowledge into his brain. "I said that," he murmured. "Yes. I did. But I don't know. I think they can make you forget things when they want to."

"Who? Those who put the bomb on you?" Rahel abruptly turned away and went to the door, which opened just before she got there. A folder was thrust in. She took it opened, read. Then spun about and walked back to Lukas.

"Your DNA came back."

Lukas dropped his hands and waited.

"You aren't in any data base," Rahel said.

"So, we still don't know who I am."

"We don't know who you are," Rahel said, "but we know who this is." She waved the folder.

"I don't understand," Lukas said.

"There is someone out there with your exact same DNA."

The Fourth Floor: The Institute

"Neuroimaging techniques of today have illuminated and confirmed the importance of Jaynes' hypothesis." Robert Olin, M.D., Ph.D., Professor Emeritus in Preventive Medicine, Karolinska Institute, Stockholm, Sweden, in *Lancet*

LARA WAKES UP WITH Sam-I-Am on top of her, his heavy black boot pressing hard on her ankle and his clammy hand over her mouth and he's humming, *'I shot a man in Reno just to watch him die'*.

Then he stops humming. "Don't scream or I'll kill you. I just want a taste."

Lara nods and stares into the glint in his eye so that he can see that she won't scream. That's all the edging she can manage, and it's not even that, its just desperate pleading that anyone is capable of.

Sam-I-Am takes his hand away and she gasps. "Please, please, move your foot. It's on my ankle."

He moves it and the relief she feels is so great that she nearly passes out. But, she doesn't and she spreads her legs wider to help him get it over with.

Lara realizes that everyone here has had to give him a taste and while she still doubts she killed her family, she knows with all her heart that one day she will kill Sam-I-Am. She turns her head, closes her eyes, and gets it over with. The only real thing she feels is that her ankle is fine. She calms her heart rate and soothes herself by thinking of all the ways possible to kill him.

He doesn't take long. Rapists never do and Lily wonders for the hundredth time that day—*how do I know that?*

He gets off of her and she feels the gasp of air return to constricted lungs and the awful weight and feel of him being gone. He uses her sink to splash water on his face. Her mirror to comb his thinning hair back into place. He zips up and buckles and leans down and wipes the blood from her torn ankle off his boot, by rubbing it against the thin sheet of her bed. Now presentable, he goes to the door and unlocks it.

Lara finally speaks. "I'm going to kill you. I just really need you to know that."

Sam-I-Am doesn't even turn. He just says in that harsh voice, "Not in this lifetime."

Lara starts to feel him trickle out between her legs and she curls herself into a tiny ball and forces herself back to sleep and like some gift, it comes.

* * *

I'm leaning by the gate to Martha's place, it's opening, and I see Jake in his truck coming to get me. His smile is a beautiful smile now--he's happy to see me. I begin to walk toward him and my ankle doesn't even hurt.

I walk over to Jake's truck and hop into the passengers seat. I turn to look at the truck bed and sigh when I see the footlocker. Well, that moment of happiness didn't last long.

I thought you were hurt, he says and I think yeah, I was but I don't feel any of it anymore, not even Sam-I-Am, but I'm not forgetting him and I will kill him.

Jake turns the truck in the turnaround next to the gate and begins the long slow crawl on the gravel road. I remember a song—'Car Wheels on a Gravel Road' and don't remember who sang it but that she had a husky voice sorta like Sam-I-Am's but hers was sad. I'm feeling a bit sad myself and really wishing that Jake didn't have a footlocker in that truck bed. He obviously is not Jim, just looks like him or whichever way you cared to think of it. I am beyond thinking about it. It's funny how much you start to not care about the weird stuff when every single thing is weird. I guess I'd find something normal to be shocking now, but I'm not sure I know what that would be or if it's even possible. All I know is that Jake really shouldn't have a footlocker in the back of his truck.

Jake's all happy. *You're just in time for dinner. Martha has made her special dish. Broiled fish and asparagus.*

That's not even a dish. A dish is a bunch of stuff covered with melted cheese and I would love some carbs covered in fat right about now but I don't think that's ever the specialty here. And beggars can't be choosers. I wish I could remember more stuff about my life except for trite sayings and clichés. No wonder they're clichés; you can't wipe them out even with a major head trauma or amnesia or insane.

I pinch my arm to see if I'm awake and it hurts. But I don't think I'm awake. Maybe I'm just sitting in some chair drooling a bit and staring out a window with dead eyes, focused on my own delusions. Or I'm really here. I decide to play it like the Fourth Floor; I am here. People say take it one day at a time so what I have to do is take it one minute at a time. It could be worse.

Really?

Maybe I'll think of how soon. I can hear the footlocker sliding around behind us and it's beyond creepy because I can only think of how tight a body would be jammed inside that to fit.

What's in there? I say.

Oh, just all my gear, I'm a volunteer firefighter.

I feel a bit better cause I can't imagine anyone who'd be kind enough to put out your fire for free would be selfish enough to chop you up and stick you in there. And I'm not a college student. Or I hope I'm not. Maybe a semester or two of community college, but according to that ID and Seth, I was only in high school. George Washington High School at that, which seemed to produce an inordinate amount of crazy killers and I wonder how I know the word inordinate, which is a relatively sane thing to wonder about.

I think.

This isn't Jim I remind myself and Martha is making dinner and she's not Maria. *Do you like to play cards?*

No, not at all.

Does Martha?

Nope. Why do you ask?

No reason and I feel a bit better. He pulls into the perfect garage and I see there are two muddy rubber boots by the back door. The last time I was here, it was nighttime and I didn't see much. It's a pristine place carved out of the forest and surrounded by a twelve-foot high fence. Perfect grass, perfect shrubs, sorta like Disneyworld if your house was in the middle of it.

A tall blond woman with deeply tanned skin, leathery actually, walks out of a door and picks up the boots.

Jake waves at her as he speaks to me. *That's Joan, one of the weeders. They use the bathroom in there,* and points to the corner of the garage as if I didn't see where she came out of. I notice she carried the boots out to the driveway before putting them on and then she was out of sight. No, howdy-do there. What's this world, dream, coming to?

What do you do, Jake, besides volunteer?

Oh, me? Not much. I'm retired. Take care of the grounds, the heavy stuff, put out fires when they call, that sort of thing. Martha makes all the money. She's a writer.

Really, what does she write?

Oh, romance stuff. You know girl with a heart of gold meets the billionaire who is her prince? That sorta stuff.

Well, it looks like that pays well, I mutter to myself.

Yeah, women do love their fantasies, he says and leads me to the door into the house, not the one Joan had come out of. I don't love my fantasies so much but there's been no billionaire yet for me, not even in my dreams. Seems fantasies and real dreams are two very different things. Just gross Sam-I-Am and cute Seth who likes hammers as much as girls.

He says, *Take off your boots.* He pulls his off and I notice I have a hole in my sock and my big toe is poking out. Really? Can't even have good socks in a delusion? It looks ridiculous because I do have the long toes and I pull them off and stuff them in the boots. The boots I've never seen before.

He leads me into the kitchen as if I'd never been there but to him I haven't been here in a year, but I slept here last night. I am tired; it's been a long day, even if it's all just a dream. I think of that great mattress and it makes me happy. So, I am adapting. The kitchen smells good and Martha heaps up the plates and we all sit after I wash my hands and she says, *So, what have you been up to all this time, Lily? And why did you just run off like that? Jake was making his famous oatmeal and when I went to wake you, you were just gone.*

A part of me just wants to tell the truth. But, it might not be the truth that I did have my oatmeal soon after I woke up in that lock down unit of the institution. Or, that I got moved to the Fourth Floor and had lunch with people who look just like you but are so not at all like you, and then I got lost in a forest and raped and now I'm here. Simple.

But, not being stupid, even in a dream, I say, *My mother lives in Seattle.* In my head, I gave her Dr. Jenkins's eyes. *Anyway, I couldn't sleep and thought I needed to stop running away from my problems so I left and hitched home and I've been there with her till she died.*

As I said it I knew it was too far, but all of this was too far, so what was one more?

Oh, dear, Martha says, her fork stopping midway. *I'm so very sorry, Lily. What happened?*

She had MS. It was always just a matter of time. This was getting easier. *My dad left years ago and the bank took the house and I've been wandering around. You were so nice to me before, I thought maybe you'd help me out again.*

Martha laid her fork down. *Here's the deal. I'm not fond of people who just leave without a note or a call for over a year and then show up wanting food and shelter. And I don't know if I believe you and I don't even know if Lily Cole is your real name.*

Join the club I think to myself and eat more of what was actually delicious asparagus while waiting for the hammer to fall.

There's always a hammer, whether it's Sam-I-Am on top, or Jake the truck driver, or the rain, or the storm, or the blood trail in the kitchen going into wherever-it-is-I-don't-want-to-go, or Seth with a real hammer.

What I am willing to do right now is you can stay in the cottage on the north end of the property and work to earn your keep.

I see Jake smile knowingly and I think earning your keep is a prominent theme in Martha's world.

You can start working with Joan in the morning. Jake says you met her.

If saw is met, indeed.

They start at eight sharp. She'll show you what to do. You'll get twenty dollars an hour and can buy food. There's a small kitchen.

I instantly see my dreams of that great mattress wither away, although the sheets aren't so hot. Martha looks at me with an odd look that has just enough crazy Maria in it for me to feel rather uncomfortable. She says, *Joan has a crew of two other women so you'll be bottom of the ladder to start but you can work your way up around here with initiative and it's spring and the weeds are going nuts.*

Weird it was just summer here and winter in the Institution. I wonder if I've already pulled the weeds or if I haven't pulled any at all. *Jake will show you the cabin.* And just like that, I know I'm dismissed. I fold my napkin and get up. I have a funny feeling that I'm only still here cause I did make that bed. Which I didn't make, but let's not get all nuts here. I start to laugh with an edge of hysteria to it that any normal person would find discomfiting.

Martha, not quite sure how normal she is, looks up at me. *Are you OK?*

Yes, I'm fine, I'm just so grateful. I've been rather discombobulated lately.

Well, Lily, you are young and you have some time to learn that life is hard but we just try and make the best of it.

Yes, yes, we do, make the best of it. Jake leads and I follow him out the front door into the most beautiful garden I've ever seen. We tug our boots on. Somehow, I know that I've never seen anything this splendid even if I have been to Disneyland. Perfect. I'd be scared to even get close to it and while it's beautiful, there's something about it that doesn't invite me to get close.

It's not my garden. It's Martha's. I don't know how I know that, but then how do I know anything?

Jake leads me past the garden onto a trail that winds through the perfectly maintained forest and says, *I've checked your Facebook page. You haven't updated it in over a year.*

Dying mom and all, I say and then I see the cottage and whatever I'd imagined yeah, that was wrong. The place is as gorgeous as the house and so charming that I want to weep. Window boxes, trellis and hundreds and hundreds of tulip bulbs making their way to the sun. Suddenly it occurs to me that I love tulips. It's the surest memory that I've experienced in the last few days or year or seven months or whatever time it is to whomever I happen to be speaking with. There's a cute rabbit made of concrete and covered in lichen and Jake lifts it up and hand me a key. *The place is yours for a while, Lily. Try to do a good job.* He turns away. *I gotta wash the dishes.*

I look at the key in my hand and realize that I can't remember having a key. Other people, Mike, Sam-I-Am, Doctor Jenkins, they've always had the key.

I unlock the door and step inside and it's really warm and charming and the couches are white canvas and I just drop on one. I'm exhausted.

Too late. I realize that falling asleep during a dream never turns out well.

This is all so hard.

Black Site, The Negev Desert

"We sometimes think, and even like to think, that the two greatest exertions that have influenced mankind, religion and science, have always been historical enemies, intriguing us in opposite directions. But this effort at special identity is loudly false. It is not religion but the church and science that were hostile to each other. And it was rivalry not contravention. Both were religious. They were two giants fuming at each other over the same ground. Both proclaimed to be the only way to divine intervention. It was a competition that first came into absolute focus with the late Renaissance, particularly in the imprisonment of Galileo in 1633." Julian Jaynes

"THE PROBLEM," RAHEL SAID, turning the folder so he could see the picture, "is that you are not identical twins. That makes no sense, since you have identical DNA. And even identical twins rarely have the exact same DNA."

Lukas's pulse raced when he saw the girl and he automatically adjusted, slowing it, then realized he wasn't sure how he knew to control his heart rate.

But he could. "I am *We*." He nodded at the picture. "That's her. Who I am to protect."

"Her name is Lily Cole," Rahel said. "Sixteen years old. The other problem." Rahel snapped the folder shut. "Is that your sister is currently in a high-security mental institution under lockdown because she murdered her family. Which is even more confusing, is that there is no mention of you as part of her family. Although it does say she killed a younger brother."

Lukas had to sit down on the edge of the gurney. "What?"

"So, you are not twins," Rahel said. "But you have identical DNA. There is some debate among the scientists, but the odds of two people having the same DNA is astronomical. Impossible some say. It is more likely the test results have been corrupted. Except you also recognize her."

"Her name is not Lily Cole," Lukas said. "It's Lara."

"Lara what?"

"I don't know."

"Is she your sister?"

"I don't know."

"Is she your clone?"

Lukas was surprised at the question. "I don't know."

"Who are you?" Rahel came to the gurney and sat next to Lukas. Not touching, but close enough that he could feel her warmth. "You're caught with a suicide vest, which you didn't detonate. You also were aware enough to defuse the cell phone detonator. But you were still there in that market with the means to kill many people. Now you tell me you're a warrior supposed to protect someone. Who turns out to have your exact same DNA, but doesn't look like you. And who has been arrested for murdering her family. And is, apparently, crazy. Who are you, Lukas? The best guess we have is that you and her are clones. Grown from the same material. Except the scientists can't account for the difference in appearance. You should be identical." Rahel leaned close, her voice low, lips next to Lukas's ear. "Start talking or it's going to get bad."

"I have to get to her," Lukas said.

"You're not getting out of here," Rahel said. "You need to understand that. But if you help us, it's not so bad."

Lukas turned and looked at her. "'Not so bad'? You've been here too long."

"Let me help you," Rahel said.

Lukas indicated the folder. "Take me to her."

"Why?"

"So I can protect her."

"From who?"

"Death," Lukas said.

"This Legion you mentioned?"

"Yes."

"I thought he was coming here."

Lukas frowned. "He is."

"You have to understand, Lukas," Rahel said, using his name for the first time, "that there's too many loose ends to your story. Too much that's strange. That makes people here very nervous. They start thinking in terms of conspiracies. This place where this girl you call Lara, but whose real name is Lily Cole, is being held? It's a part of a black site, just like this place. Which means someone in the United States government thinks there's more to her than just a murdered family."

"Where in the United States?" Lukas asked.

The door burst open and four men strode into the room. Large, masked men, emitting emptiness.

Rahel stood up, getting out of the way as the men grabbed Lukas and threw him back down on the gurney and strapped him in.

Lukas stared at her as she walked to the door. She looked over her shoulder once at him, and then she was gone.

And then it got bad.

The Fourth Floor

I am emphasizing individuals set apart from others as ill, because, according to our theory, we could say that before the second millennium B.C., everyone was schizophrenic." Julian Jaynes

LARA WAKES UP AND she's still curled into a ball on the thin mattress of the cell on the Fourth Floor.

She pulls the blanket over her head and wishes with all her might to be back in the cottage. Her ankle hurts and she can feel the wetness of the blood where Sam-I-Am's boot peeled back some skin. She's still sore and aching and thinks of all the ways she can kill him. After ten minutes of wishing for the cottage and how to kill Sam-I-Am, she knows she's going to be here a while.

She gets up and makes the bed because that seems as ingrained in her as silly expressions. She uses the metal sink to clean as much as she can and there's a small plastic bag of toothbrush, paste, a comb and some cream. She finds clean clothes in the locker and gets dressed. Some flip flops and a gray, rough pantsuit thing. It doesn't feel great but it's not the soiled jeans, so she feels better. Her feet look pretty good in the flip flops and she goes to the door and tries the knob and it's unlocked so she walks down the dark hall to the cafeteria and smells bacon and knows it's breakfast. Her world is rapidly shrinking down to mealtimes, which still have significance. She gets pancakes, scrambled eggs, a lot of bacon and a few sausages because she's so hungry. Seems fish and asparagus don't last long as sustenance.

At least its not oatmeal.

She sees Jim and Maria but they seem engrossed in the same argument and when Claude waves her over she goes and sits across from him.

"Where's Seth?" Lara asks.

"Oh, he doesn't like breakfast. He killed his girlfriend in the back of a Denny's after a Grandslam."

"Oh, pancakes and hammers." She isn't even surprised anymore.

Claude glances at her tray and says, "You ain't gonna look so hot in that jumpsuit if you're gonna eat like that."

"I have a very high metabolism," she says. She wants to add it's so fast that I live a year in a day. And who wants to look hot here anyway? She squirms a bit in her seat and Claude leans over and whispers, "Did Sam take a taste?"

When she says nothing he adds, "Well he won't do it again so you're good to go there."

Lara is no longer hungry and puts the slice of bacon back on her plate. "Why do you guys let him get away with that, cause really, it's not like we're a roomful of doormats here."

Claude smiles. "It's the barred windows and the locked doors and steel cages and then he has a gun of course. You can't see it. He keeps it inside his shirt. He's also got a sap and he's faster with that than most of us with our fists."

To Lara, it sounded as if he knew of what he spoke. He shovels some drippy eggs in his mouth and a bit of yolk slides down his chin and she turns away.

"But why don't you do something? Complain? File a report? There's gotta be something."

Claude wipes the egg off with the back of one hand and half covers a burp. "Because no one will believe us. Come on you're one of us. You've lied your whole life and gotten away with it till now cause people didn't know what you were and now they do and so they don't believe jack shit no more from us and I guess it is their payback."

"Well, I'm going to kill him," Lara says.

Claude leans forward again and says, "no, no, no, we do not kill Sam. It's sort of a mutual psycho agreement cause I've been here awhile and so have a lot of these murdering sons of bitches and Sam ain't the worst we've seen. He just wants one taste and then he leaves you alone, so we let him slide. It's what we're good at." He stares in her eyes as if for reassurance that she won't break the psychopath code.

Lara ponders a sausage link wondering if she can eat it. "So that's it; he only rapes us once, so good to go?"

"Shit, yeah," Claude says.

Lara picks up the link and takes a bite. It tastes pretty good.

Claude asks, "You gonna eat that bacon?"

"Yes, yes I am." She forces herself to live in the moment as she'd done with Jake in the truck. "So, what do you know about Jim?"

Claude slops some more egg about. "Footlocker Jim?"

"Yeah, him. Did he do something else aside from chopping up girls and stuffing them in footlockers?"

Claude's face turns grim. It's not a good thing for Lara to see and she says, "Know what? You can have my bacon."

That doesn't stop Claude. "He said they only got him on that one girl. That's his story and he's sticking to it, so we all do too. Got it?"

"Yeah." Lara nods. "I do get that."

And then Claude starts to laugh. "I put the hammock up two months ago." He finishes laughing with himself and says, "I think Jim was a fireman or an ambulance guy or something. You know those guys who save cats and shock your heart back to life? Something like that."

Lara forces a smile, cause really, what else was she going to do? "A caring, helping member of his community?"

Claude snorts and rubs his face with a paper napkin, which is two drippy egg yolks. "Yeah, caring member of the community till he cut one girl's head off."

"Right. One. The number is one." She starts to eat the pancakes but they'd turned rubbery. She wishes she'd kept the bacon.

Claude gets a sly look on his face and says, "Know what your nickname is?"

Lara doesn't want to know but she's living in the moment. "I don't have a clue."

He says, "it's Lily Squared. You know Lizzie Borden, who killed her parents?"

Lara realized that yes, she did know about Lizzie Borden. Other than the Li, she doesn't see the leap from Lily to Lizzie. "But she only killed her parents."

"That's why you're Lily Squared," Claude says with the certainty of crazy logic.

Lily feels a bit sick thinking of people sitting around giving her a name based on killing a mother, father and a sister and a brother, whom she absolutely doesn't even remember.

"Pretty wicked," Claude says. "Did you do it while they were sleeping? Cause even a ten-year-old boy could fight you off."

"Yeah, they were sleeping," she says and tries very hard to think of a home in the dark and her in those jeans and that ironed shirt walking from room to room with a big knife.

Nothing.

Claude leans even closer till she can smell the egg on his breath, which would soon start to smell, like sulfur and says, "You reliving it right now?"

She looks at him with all the earnest muster she can force up. "No, I'm not reliving it. I don't remember it. There's nothing there. Actually there's nothing in my head. I don't even think my name is Lily."

Claude leans back in his chair so quickly that it creaks ominously and reminds her of Dr. Jacobson's suffering chair. "You really don't remember anything You're not trying a scam? Cause we don't rat on each other here."

"No, not one thing. It's like I was born a week ago downstairs and now I'm here."

"Jeez kid, I think you're on the wrong floor." Suddenly he looks at her with suspicion because he's let her in thinking she was one of the gang and he knows if she were one of the gang not only would those memories be there--they'd be replayed for further enjoyment. "Are you a spy, some plant? Is that why you're asking about footlocker Jim?"

"No," she backtracks. And for the first time, even beyond what Sam had done, Lara feels fear and she can tell that Claude smells it on her as easily as she smells his eggs. She sees his nostrils flare for a moment like a wild animal on a hunt for something more substantial than eggs. She tries to calm herself and imagines the clean, perfect garage, the rubber boots with the mud on them.

Just as suddenly, he too relaxes, shaking his head sadly. "You aint one of us. Try to keep that hidden, but you won't be able to do that for long around the rest. This is not good." He actually seems concerned for her, which is rather depressing.

Claude leans forward and she can smell the food on his breath, which is as disturbing as his words. "Who are you, kid? If you aint one of us?"

"I'm one of you," Lara says. "Lizzie Squared, remember?"

Claude shakes his head and speaks in a low voice. "This place. It's the government. I think the CIA or one of them other alphabet soup organizations. The ones who run Area 51. Super-secret stuff."

Claude looks around as if everyone cares about this crazy conversation rather than their own crazy conversations.

"Aliens?" Lara asked, trying to play along, get along.

Claude pulls back. "Get real."

"Right."

Claude picks up his tray. And he walks away and Lara takes a few gulps of air and tries to keep her mind in the garage. But then she sees Jake's white truck, the footlocker in the bed and opens her eyes and whispers to herself *live in the moment live in the moment* and she relaxes a bit. And then she thinks—*I didn't kill them.*

She decides that Claude is a much better diagnostician than Dr. Jacobson. Because really, it takes one to know one. Except his paranoia taints things.

Suddenly she's exhausted and walks out but does take her tray up because tidy is bone deep. She passes Sam in the hallway. He doesn't even look at her and she opens her door, which is still unlocked and falls on the bed and pulls the thin blanket back over her head.

She's no longer sure the dreams are worse the reality.

The Negev Desert

"As the deer pants for streams of water, so my soul pants for you, my God." Psalm 42.

THE BEDOUINS CALL dust devils *Jinn*. Spirits of the desert that can assume human or animal form. And once they do, they have supernatural power over mere mortals. On the other side of the world, the Navajo call them *Chiindi*, the spirits of their ancestors. If it spins clockwise, it is a good spirit. The other way? Not so good. A demon.

The man watched a dust devil spinning to his left front, picking up sand, catching it in the whirlwind, and dancing across the desert floor. He was dressed in loose black shirt and pants, and was barefoot. A strip of black cloth was wrapped around his head, leaving only a slit for his eyes. A leather belt was cinched around his waist holding two sheathed daggers; handles tilted forward, one on each hip. His hands rested lightly on the hilts of the weapons as he tracked the dust devil, the landscape lit by the stars and quarter moon.

He liked this place. It reminded him of where he came from. Barren, unforgiving, harsh.

The word Negev evolved from the word *dry* in Hebrew. Averaging less than 200 milliliters (or one cup) of rain per year, the area lives up the name. Despite containing over half of Israel's terrain, it held less than ten percent of its population.

After being banished from Egypt, Abraham made the Negev his home for a bit, before moving on, which indicated a degree of wisdom. Moses sent scouts into the Negev during the Exodus, and then didn't go there.

More wisdom.

The dust devil dissipated and was gone. The man shifted his attention, scanning the land ahead, slowly discerning the anti-intrusion and detection devices in the space in front of him.

Impressive.

And from what he knew of those who controlled the facility that held his target, they didn't put all their trust in technology. Always wise. Nothing was more effective than a well-trained person.

The man-in-black reached up and pulled the strip of cloth across his nose down and sniffed the night air. Then he put it back in place. He knelt on one knee, lowering his head, and closing his eyes.

Searching.

* * *

Three hundred meters to his left front an Israeli commando in a hide site was peering through a night vision scope on top of a sniper rifle, the latest version rolled out by his country just the previous year. Top of the line, able to effectively reach out 1,200 meters, three-quarters of a mile, but among the trained snipers, they were confident that could hit and kill out to a mile with special ammunition that featured heavy, depleted uranium cores.

The sniper, guarding one of Israeli's most important secrets, had the special ammunition. His bunker was built into the side of a rock and sand strewn ridge, a half-mile outside the perimeter of the Black Site. It was built with reinforced concrete and entered through a hatch in the rear, with just a firing slit in the front.

He was midway through a four-hour shift, scanning his sector, never repeating the same pattern. It was boring work, but he was completely focused.

* * *

The man-in-black opened his eyes and stood. Then he began to run, bare feet lightly touching sand and rock, bent slightly forward at the waist, following the terrain, keeping to the lowest part of the land, but as he went faster his body started flickering in and out of sight as if time were a strobe and he was moving in the blank spots in between.

* * *

The sniper squinted, catching a glimpse of something moving. He quartered the area, trying to discern what had caught his attention. He switched from night vision to thermal.

Flickering images of something, but then nothing.

He'd seen dust devils before at night. This was different. He considered calling it in, but what could he call in? 'Something' was out there?

Besides, he had an AN/PRS-9A Anti-Intrusion System arrayed in front of his position that monitored acoustic and seismic activity and was capable of picking up vehicles a quarter mile away and a person within a hundred yards. Layered on top of that was a system of infrared and magnetic sensors that could provide additional information about anything coming this way.

The best technology in the world. Nothing could get past it.

He pulled his eye back from the scope, glanced down.

All green.

Nothing.

He looked outside. It was there, for just an instant, then gone. Then there again. Barely a form. Something.

And it was moving fast, so fast, he lost track of it. And then it wasn't there at all. He scanned the sector carefully, flipping between night vision and thermal.

Nothing.

The anti-intrusion receiver glowed green.

Strange.

What was even stranger was he felt no pain as an extraordinarily sharp blade severed his trigger hand from his body. The fingers reflexively tightened around the grip, but, as was the standard 'my finger is my safety' mantra of special operations soldiers the world over, the trigger finger had been resting alongside the trigger guard, not on the trigger itself, so the rifle didn't fire.

The sniper's good hand let go of the useless weapon as he spun about. Instinct ruled and he reached for his pistol, nerves firing to where they no longer existed in his wrist.

The reality he had no hand to draw the gun blossomed along with pain. But he was already adjusting, scrambling across his body with his off hand as he tried to discern who was attacking him.

Just a dark figure was in the bunker with him, moonlight glinting off a bloodied blade held ready, but not striking to finish things.

The sniper ripped open the cover on the holster.

"No guns," the dark figure said, the blade flicking forward so fast, the sniper couldn't track. He felt the pain though as the blade slit the back of his remaining hand. He pulled it away, pressing his back against the front of the bunker, trying to make sense of this bewildering situation.

"Who are you?" the sniper demanded. He was slowly lifting his hand, no sudden movement, to switch on the transmit for his throat mike.

The blade was much faster, darting forward, slicing the wire connecting it to the transmitter in its pouch on the combat vest.

"No radio."

The sniper glanced at the stub, at the blood pulsing out. A part of his mind knew he needed a tourniquet, but . . .

"My regrets for taking your strong hand," the man-in-black said. "But I could not risk a shot being fired. It also makes this not much of a challenge. You may draw your knife for honor if you wish."

"What?" The sniper was confused, but he took the opening, sliding his commando dagger out of its sheath, holding it awkwardly in a hand not used to wielding it.

The man-in-black sheathed one of the blades. He reached up and pulled the black cloth away from his mouth and lifted the blooded dagger to his lips. His tongue darted out like a snake's, licking it clean. "Sweet is the taste of the life of a warrior."

"Who are you?"

"My name is Legion, for we are many." He replaced the cloth, leaving only his eyes clear.

The sniper belatedly reacted as a blade flashed, but the damage was already done as his dagger reached a defensive posture. A trickle of blood slid down from the slide along one cheek.

"It is a sign of courage to fight even when there is no hope," Legion said. "To fight even as life drains away. If I had the time . . ." he fell silent as if mourning the lack of time.

Running out of blood and options, the sniper charged, jabbing with the dagger. And struck nothing.

Pain exploded along his back as a slit was opened through his body armor, his shirt, and into the flesh, but not deeply. Barely an eighth of an inch, evenly cut, as precise as a surgeon.

The sniper turned, acceptance beginning to outweigh the pain. He briefly wondered what kind of knife could cut through the armor, but really, was that important now?

"It is our art," Legion said. He wiggled the blade. "This is our brush and your body is the canvas."

The sniper began to murmur a prayer in Hebrew. He lowered the hand with the dagger, and then the fingers went slack. It clattered to the concrete floor of the bunker.

Legion was disappointed. "There is no art in slaughter."

He slashed the sniper's throat, a clean cut that blossomed a cascade of blood.

The sniper went to his knees, and then keeled over, thudding onto the floor.

Legion climbed out of the bunker and looked ahead into the darkness. There was a glow on the horizon. The security lights surrounding the black site.

"I am Legion, for we are many," he whispered.

Lara

"The unlocatable location of things thought about." **Julian Jaynes**

I WAKE UP TO A FIRM knocking on the door. My face is stuck with saliva to the clean white canvas of the couch. I peek out the window above it and see Joan in the boots, standing tall with purposeful intention. I open the door.

She looks at me. *Wow, you're a hard sleeper.*

She makes it sound as if sleeping is one of the deadly sins, which I find weirdly amusing, given, what all. I touch my cheek where her focus is and I feel the lines of the rough couch cover etched into my face. I wipe some drool off my chin. *Yeah, I was really tired. Give me five minutes, okay and I'll be out.*

You better eat some breakfast, she says and I say, *No, I actually already ate.*

She frowns and looks about. *What did you eat?*

I can feel the pancake and sausage doing a slow dance. It's sorta surprising to me how nuts I am because I feel pretty good. You know in an insane sort of way?

With no answer forthcoming, she hands me my boots with the torn sock still in them. *You left these outside, but not on the tray where they belong. Don't do that again.*

Another sin that I can't remember.

I grab them and run off to pee and tell her, *I'll be right out.*

Instead, she walks in and surveys the room. It's all-pretty perfect just like I found it, at least I think so, but she zooms right in on the damp part of the cushion. "Better clean that up. Martha won't like it. You should have slept in the bed. That's what it's for."

Glad she clarifies the whole bed thing for me.

I say, *Sorry, sorry but I was so tired.*

Joan huffs. *I got forty years on you. What do you have to be tired about?*

Geez, Claude's an easier guy than her and I shake my head like some dog trying to explain why he ate that favorite house slipper and she gives me one hint with her blue eyes that I may go and do my business. I shut the bathroom door and squat over the toilet and pee for a very long time. It's an odd thing; I only squat over perfect toilets. I flush the toilet and it's another good one that barely makes a sound. There is a calligraphy card, of course, warning the user. I pull open a drawer and find the same pack of toothbrushes; Martha must buy them by the case. There's also a good hairbrush and even a scrunchie. When I come back out feeling pretty good about how normal I almost look I see that Joan has the couch cushion at the sink and is rubbing it with some water.

Guilt projected through action.

I grab my boots and walk onto the porch and sit on the bench under the window and turn the sock so my big toe doesn't stick out and lace up my boots and when she walks back out I'm ready and smile and say, *What now?*

Because really, what the fuck now? I have tried so hard to live in the moment but occasionally you do have to know what the next moment is.

She shuts the door, locks it with a key on her own keychain, and says; *Now we work.*

I'm really longing for a dream where I just get to do nothing.

She's got some long legs and walks fast and talks without turning her head so it's hard to hear her. *I sense you are a troubled young girl, Lily.*

For the first time I really want to say my name is Lara but I don't for some reason. I'm in the moment. She gets to the edge of the walk and picks up a bright yellow bucket, the color of the yolks smeared all over Claude's napkin and with it are some work gloves and a metal fork thing with a wooden handle.

Joan hands me the bucket and says, *You can start right here.*

I look down where last night or some night I just saw new tulips and now I see weeds everywhere amidst the flowers, sticking their heads out of the deep reddish mulch.

I sense you are in pain, Lily, she says to me. *You know what the only anodyne for pain is?*

And oddly enough, I know what an anodyne is and I know the answer. *Work?*

Exactly. She's not impressed I know what anodyne is, but I am. Small victories.

I grab the bucket and she says, *I'll be back for you at lunch. We eat at noon on the gazebo. Martha provides lunch.*

My heart starts to sink. *She does? How nice of her.*

Damn right it's nice, Joan says. *She orders in sandwiches from the deli every day. She doesn't need to do that.*

I'm immediately filled with joy at the thought of a real sandwich and she stalks off like she were a Roman soldier looking forward to taking

Gaul. She turns back to add—*Get the roots.* And I put on my gloves and start to weed. After an hour or so, I'm thinking that ripping out weeds might be the most relaxing, satisfying thing ever.

There's a real thrill to digging down with the weeder and extracting the entire root out with one pull. The bucket is filled to the brim and I've stomped it down a few times and suddenly Joan is back. *Lunch.*

She looks around. *Not bad.*

I suddenly feel prouder than I have in a week or a year or seven months depending on the lay of the land and she adds *For a beginner.*

And I think maybe I'm not a beginner at all? If Claude says I didn't kill my family, maybe I didn't and I can see that Joan is impressed though she's not the type to throw you a real bone. Maybe I'm an orphan and got to 18 without one family ever wanting me and I went out on my own and turned into a professional weeder? Weirder things have happened. She grabs my bucket, which is much heavier than she thought, I can see it on her face, and she says, *I'll empty it for you. Leave your gloves. We got a place to wash our hands.*

And I follow her taking great pleasure in how heavy the bucket is.

The Institution

*"The mind is still haunted with its old unconscious ways; it broods on
lost authorities; and the yearning, the deep and hollowing yearning for
divine volition and service is with us still."* Julian Jaynes

DR. JACOBSON LEANED BACK and tried to feel calm. Best way to be
with these nuts. These dangerous-manipulative-cheating-horrible-steal-
your-life nuts. He glanced at Claude but tried not to look too long. The
way you never challenge a strange dog by looking it in the eye.

Jacobson adjusted himself amidst of the screeching of the chair and
tried to appear as professional as he can but he's disturbed by Claude's
slight smile of the lion staring at prey. And Sam, the worst human to ever
work in a hospital, has his same expression of life-sucks-and-then-*you*-die,
but he's here to protect him from this killing machine so Jacobson tried to
ignore him.

He says with as much gravitas as is allowed him. "So, Claude. Why
did you want to see me?"

Claude leaned forward and Jacobson mirrored him, leaning back and
the chair squealed. "Geez, Doc you need to lose a few pounds or that chair
is gonna run away some night."

Jacobson flinched; he hated to be called Doc. It reminded him of
being five with that step-mother who fed him burnt grilled cheese
sandwiches everyday for lunch while he tried to stay small and un-
annoying by watching Bugs Bunny all day. He wondered why Claude had
been allowed down here to see him; definitely not protocol. He hadn't
seen Claude since intake. Claude had been sent to the Fourth Floor
immediately, no stopping, no two-hundred dollars for passing Go, but
whisked right up there. What the hell was he doing down here?

"What do you want?"

Claude spoke slowly. "That girl, Lily Cole, the one you sent to us on
the Fourth Floor? She doesn't belong there. She didn't do it. You know:
kill her family."

Jacobson sensed the manipulative fingers of Dr. Jenkins reaching down to fuck with him. Did she expect him to buy into this bullshit and make a protest about the transfer order on Lily Cole? Women.

He glanced at Sam and that face. It was the face of a bored man reading a boring book in a boring house on a boring street in a boring town. Maybe that was actually a clinical manifestation of lack of affect. Jacobson made a mental note to check on that but he knew he wouldn't, even while he was noting it. He looked back to Claude who did have affect. It wasn't pleasant but it was there. Not a good one.

"So," Jacobson said, pressing his fingers together under one of his chins, a pose he used to practice in front of a mirror. Back when he had a practice. "You know this how? Are they teaching a forensic course on the Fourth Floor that I'm unaware of?"

Claude gave him a look that told him exactly how unaware he thought the doctor was about anything and Jacobson started to smell burnt cheese.

"Doc, she didn't do it. She can't. I know that."

Jacobson felt emboldened, having smoked out Jenkins's ploy. "Did *you* do it? Is that how you know?" He saw a look of revulsion and disgust slide across Claude's face and realized that he'd been much happier in the moment playing the game with Jeannie. Psychopaths are actually quite thrilling and entertaining while you're their target and they're hiding. But when they realize you know who they are, they become something entirely different and drop the mask, letting you know how revolting you are to them.

"I don't kill kids, Doc. That's gross. You read my file. I killed old people whose time was up. And only when the old lady said it was okay. Keep up, here, all right?"

"What old lady?"

"Stay on topic, Doc."

"So what is the issue here?" Jacobson asked.

"She's a kid and she's not one of us and she didn't do it and she ain't gonna fit in and when that happens she's gonna get hurt. Worse than she's already been hurt." Claude turned and looked at Sam for a second and not one nerve on Sam's face moved. Jacobson felt completely outside of whatever was passing between those two and for that he was grateful.

"So, you're here to tell me that a girl on the Fourth Floor who killed her family didn't do it because *you* don't think she's capable of it?"

"Yeah, exactly," Claude said.

Jacobson snorted. "So, maybe you should write up a dissenting opinion? I'll send it to Doctor Jenkins. Then you can get a white coat and a nametag and you can give us all your professional opinion on everyone."

Psychopaths are actually rather literal creatures and Claude said, "Just the thing about Lily. I'll do that. I can write it if you like. I just want her off the floor. She's gonna get eaten up. And I mean that like, laterally."

Jacobson started to laugh now that he had the upper hand and there was no burning cheese smell any more and said, "Oh, fuck me Claude. You're an inmate in this fine institution for the criminally insane, to keep you locked away from the rest of us normal people, but now you believe you're a diagnostician. And it's literally, you dolt."

"The state?" Claude laughed. His eyes turned into the same tiny animal slits he's seen in Jeannie when he confronted her with the bottle of untouched Xanax. "Oh, I could fuck you doc, but I don't think my dick is long enough to get through the two feet of your ass checks. You don't even know what this place is."

Jacobson put both hands on the top of the desk and pressed down hard, trying to maintain the control that had been preached at him all through his training. But his motive wasn't to understand Claude; he was a psychopath and there's nothing to understand there.

"What is this place, Claude?" Jacobson asked in his most tightly controlled voice.

"You're a stooge," Claude said. "They needed someone real, someone who'd bear the outside scrutiny, to sit here on the first floor and sign the papers. You're the fall guy. No one else signs anything here. No one else exists here. Not Jenkins. Nobody. Just you. Your name is on everything."

Sam walked forward and put his hand on Claude's shoulder. "Let's go."

"Not yet," Jacobson said. "I'm not done with him."

Sam put his full focus on Jacobson. "Yes, you are."

Jacobson felt the chill of staring into the eyes of another psychopath, an everyday occurrence but not from an employee.

"This game is over," Sam said and it wasn't quite if it was to Claude or Jacobson.

Claude nodded. "Sure, Sam. Sure." He stood. "Take care, fat man."

Jacobson jerked up. "Get him out of here!"

Sam, not bothering to suppress a superior grin, grabbed Claude and led him out.

* * *

When they got to the elevator and Sam swiped his card, Claude was surprised to see the old woman already inside. She was dressed in a black dress, more of a robe, with a hood pulled up, hiding most of her face, and had a long set of shears in the crook of one arm. They were so long they extended over her shoulder. A great weapon but Clause had no desire to even try for them. Crazy people tend to instinctively know their limits.

Sam didn't seem to see her, shoving Claude into the elevator and scanning his card. Claude almost said something, but then it was Sam. It had been a while since Claude had seen the old woman. He nodded a greeting and she nodded back.

Old friends.

The doors slid shut.

"It is his time," the old woman said.

Sam didn't seem to hear.

They were between the second and third floors on the elevator when Claude took his handcuffed hands and looped them over Sam's head. Claude slammed the guard to the floor and knelt on his back with all his weight and slowly strangled him. He could have broken Sam's neck, but that would have been merciful.

He looked up for the old woman but she was gone.

Well that's odd, Claude thought.

Sam still had a few gasps in him when the elevator started to open on the Fourth Floor. But, he was dead by the time the doors were wide open.

Claude had hoped that the doc could see things his way but no one believed you when you were here and they knew what you were. So, he'd taken care of Sam himself so Lily wouldn't be tempted to cause he knew that regular people would do all sorts of weird things when pushed to some edge that he himself had never known.

He had a smile on his face when the men in the black body armor came racing down the hallway, weapons at the ready. As they led him away, he was still smiling because, honestly, it was the first genuinely altruistic thing he'd done since her arrived here.

Black Site, Negev Desert

"... Scientific interest in [Jaynes's] work has been re-awakened by the consistent findings of right-sided activation patterns in the brain, as retrieved with the aid of neuroimaging studies in individuals with verbal auditory hallucinations." **Jan Dirk Blom, M.D, Ph.D., in** *A Dictionary of Hallucinations*

LUKAS SAT ON THE concrete floor, his body an amalgamation of bruises and scrapes.

The beating had been brutal but controlled. He still had the broken rib, but no other bone had been broken, and the men had carefully avoided doing more damage to that spot. It had been a strange experience, violence apparently unleashed, but very carefully administered.

He'd felt nothing from the men, despite the ferocity with which they attacked.

But now he felt something. He looked up at the small hole in the ceiling of the cell. It was black, indicating night outside.

He was distracted as the door screeched open. Rahel came in, not wearing her mask and carrying a tray and a file folder.

"I warned you," Rahel said, noting his bruises.

"You did," Lukas agreed. "Will you take me to her, now?"

Rahel shook her head. "You're never getting out of here."

"I'll be out of here shortly, one way or another," Lukas said.

"What do you mean?" Rahel asked.

"He's coming," Lukas said.

"Death?" Rahel said.

Lukas nodded. "Legion. I can feel him. He's close."

"How can you feel someone?" Rahel asked. "What do you mean? How did you know about my family?" She put the tray down next to Lukas. Food, some sort of food, was smeared on it. A gray, congealed mass. "You said you were hungry."

Lukas glanced at it. "I think my hunger is a different kind of hunger."

"It's nourishing," Rahel said. "It might not look like much, but it's—"

Lukas shook his head. "Not food. I need to get to her. That's my hunger. I know that now. It is a need I cannot control. It's strange. I can control my heartbeat, but not this." He looked at Rahel. "It would be good for you to let me go before he gets here. For you to leave."

"No one can get in here," Rahel said.

"He is Legion," Lukas said. "He can get in anywhere."

"We've been studying the data on you."

"My blood?" Lukas asked.

"Your blood," Rhael said. "But much more. Your DNA. And the little we've been able to glean about the girl in America. Most amazing. Technically impossible."

"Where is she in America?" Lukas asked him.

"That's not important."

"It is to me," Lukas said.

"We didn't think it was possible for two people to have identical DNA outside of identical twins," Rahel said. "And even then, they have to be of the same sex. Even if twins mated and produced twins, the DNA would not be identical. This had to have been done in a lab. But no one is capable of that. Not yet. There are rumors the Chinese are doing human experiments. They did do the glow in the dark pigs a few years ago. But you're almost an adult. This had to have been done years ago. You had to have been done years ago."

"Done how?" Lukas asked.

"Sequencing, manipulation of the basic building blocks of human life. Do you remember your parents?"

Lukas frowned. "I don't remember anything before the market."

"You remember Legion and Lara," Rahel pointed out.

"That isn't memory," Lukas said.

"What is it?" Rahel asked.

"Awareness."

"I hate to tell you this," Rahel said, "but I don't think you had parents. Not in the usual sense."

Lukas absorbed that without comment.

"How did you knew about my family?" Rahel asked. "Was there something I said? Did?"

"I just knew."

"Awareness?" Rahel asked.

Lukas nodded. He reached down and took a handful of the gray mush and shoveled it in his mouth.

"Thought you weren't hungry?" Rahel asked.

"A warrior has to eat." He reached for another handful, but paused, cocking his head. "He's close." He looked up at Rahel. "If you don't let me go now, many people will die. Someone has already died."

"Who?" Rahel glanced at the door, as if expecting the men to rush back in and pick up where they left off.

Lukas shook his head. "I don't know. But there has been a death. There will be more."

"You don't seem very concerned for yourself," Rahel said.

"I am *We*," Lukas said.

"What does that mean?"

That's when a klaxon went off and red light flashed through the room.

Lara

"The king dead is a living god." Julian Jaynes

LARA SAW TWO WOMEN AND four boxed lunches under the gazebo on a long teak table. She was becoming obsessed with what she did and didn't know. She knew the table was teak. She didn't know her birthday or her real age for that matter. She knew the aft end of a boat but had no memory at all of a mother or father, much less siblings. She wasn't sure if she was awake or asleep but she remembered waking this morning on the soggy spot of the couch so maybe she was still awake. Or still dreaming.

Joan ran the lunch hour with the same crisp efficiency as she did everything else. Lara figured Joan could account for every moment of her life. She probably still knew the day and time of her first burp and it had been an excellent burp; of that, Lara was sure. There were four yellow buckets near the end of the table. All empty and Joan announced that Lara would get the extra cookie. She explained that there was a contest for poundage when Joan emptied the buckets.

Lara asked, "you have scales out there?"

Joan simply smiled. "No, I can just tell."

Well if you're going to be good at something, balls to the wall or whatever, Lara thought. One of the other women didn't seem all that welcoming, but she figured it might be because she was getting the cookie. *What a great way to meet new friends*, she thought. Joan introduced as if they were meeting for a merger between two conglomerates. *Really*, Lara *thought, conglomerate? Live in the moment. Live in the moment.*

"Sally, Jess, this is Lily."

Lara made a great effort to remember their names because who knew when she'd see them again? Sally was around Joan's age with the same weathered face of someone used to the outside and she had a single streak of white in her dark hair, which was so thick and appeared to be so long that she just knotted and held it in place with a pencil. She had a warm genuine smile and Lara liked her at once.

Jess was younger, maybe even younger than Lara. She had pale blue eyes, which gave her the look of someone always on the verge of tears. She didn't smile at all and stared back with enough direct gaze and aggression to earn her a chair in the dining room of the Fourth Floor.

As if by some silent command, they all opened their boxes and it was a very good lunch. It was the best meal, food and company wise, that Lara could remember which wasn't much but it was something and living in the moment meant honoring that moment. The three began to talk while Lara focused on eating because her delusional or not delusional breakfast was long gone. Weeding was hard and she could see the blisters forming even though the gloves were thick.

Jess stared at her. "Why are you here?" It was a demand.

Lara decided to stick to the script. "My mother just died and Martha is helping me out till I get my act together."

"And how long will that take?" Jess pushed.

Geez, Jess, Lily thought, *maybe centuries*? But she said, "Few weeks maybe" and covered her mouth in a polite gesture.

"Joan says you're staying in the cottage?" Jess asked, more stated, so Lara saw no need to reply.

Oh, that was it, Lara realized. She continued to eat.

Sally spoke up. "Oh, I'm sorry about your mother. I hope it all works out for you. This is a special place, so you're lucky for now."

"I don't feel very lucky," Lara said, truth breaking through the script.

Jess shook her head. "You are lucky. The pay is good and the work isn't bad once you get used to the stress on your back."

"Why can't we just spray all these weeds?" Lara asked and three pairs of eyes widened in shock.

"Martha would never use poison," Joan said. "It's not right."

You mean like cheating, Lara thought but she kept her mouth shut and tried to get along. The conversation was as boring as four women discussing weeds could be. After eating the extra cookie, Lara felt stuffed and suddenly very tired and her back was beginning to ache.

"When is quitting time?" she asked.

Joan said, "five."

Four more hours and Lara started to doubt she had it in her. They cleaned everything up and Joan handed out the buckets seeming to know which of the yellow buckets belonged exactly to whom. She must line them up in some order Lara thought. She trudged back to the tulips and couldn't help feeling that the folks on the Fourth Floor, while scary as shit, were much more interesting. Except for Sally. There was something fragmenting about her but a bit intriguing too and Lara decided to get to know her better if she ever saw her again.

Which was weird because right then Sally came walking up. "You've got to pace yourself."

Was this about the cookie? Lara wondered.

"Awareness of self," Sally said, stopping at the edge of the tulip bed, and folding her arms across her chest.

Lara blinked. "What?"

"Awareness of self," Sally repeated. "Then awareness of others. One, then two."

"Right." Lara was grateful for the break. Her back was really beginning to hurt and she had to wonder if it was because Jess had brought it up. She hadn't been aware of it before lunch. So there was something to being too aware.

"There's levels three and four also," Sally said.

"Right." For lack of any other response.

"Three is awareness of the world," Sally said, spreading her hands, taking in the perfectly manicured forest around them. "What do you think of Martha's domain?"

An odd choice of words, Lara thought. "Pretty."

"Controlled," Sally said. "Martha likes control. That's her flaw."

This was getting as weird as the Fourth Floor, Lara thought. She wished her dreams stayed simple. Couldn't she just weed in peace?

"Martha thinks this—" Sally indicated the tulip bed and then beyond—"is being close to the Earth Mother. Close to the essence of it. She's wrong, of course."

Of course, Lara thought, but didn't say anything.

"To worship the Earth, as she should be worshipped," Sally continued, "one must respect it as it is. Not try to shape it into what we want. We are part of it, not the other way around."

"Right." Seemed to Lara that weeding wasn't respecting the Earth. Weeds were part of it, weren't they?

"Do you think it's odd that she needs a fence around all of this?"

Lara hadn't thought of it at all. "Not really." She frowned. "Why is there a fence?"

"She says it's to keep the deer out," Sally said, as if she didn't believe that was the reason. "I'm surprised you got out of here the last time," she added. "Joan told me about it. That you were here a year ago and just disappeared."

Lara slowly got to her feet. "Is the fence to keep us in?"

Sally shrugged. "If it was, it didn't work, did it?"

"You said this was a special place at lunch," Lara said.

"You remember lunch?"

Lara tensed. "What's awareness four?"

Sally smiled, as if Lara had just grabbed the brass ring; whatever that meant. "Awareness beyond the world. The fourth awareness. Ironic isn't it? The Fourth?" She shook her head. "Oh well. I'll see you later. Maybe." She turned and walked away.

That was weird, Lara thought. Then again, what wasn't in a dream?

Lara worked hard for two more hours but then her body, weakened by who knew how many months of institutionalized care, just gave in all at once as though a switch had been turned.

She laid down on the soft mulch, careful to not disturb the fledgling tulips, thinking if she could only rest for a moment she'd be fine, but she and fine weren't even mild acquaintances.

Black Site, Negev Desert

"One does one's thinking before one knows what one is to think about." Julian Jaynes.

THE KLAXON HAD STOPPED sounding but the red light was still flashing.

"Speak to me," Rahel said. She had one hand pressed against the earpiece and Lukas wasn't sure if she was talking to him or to whoever was on the other end of her radio. "Stop with this Legion and Death bullshit. Who's attacking us?"

Lukas pointed at his own ear. "What do you hear?"

"Someone's breached the perimeter," Rahel said. "Security is on top of it."

"Is security on top of it?" Lukas asked.

"It's confusing," Rahel admitted. "If the site perimeter is breached, that meant someone got through the outer perimeter. One of the outer guards isn't reporting back."

"He's dead," Lukas said.

"How do you know all this?" Rahel walked up to him, close. So close, he could smell her.

"You're not afraid," Lukas said. "The others here, they're not afraid. But that's because they don't really know fear. They don't know much of any feeling. You're not like them. You shouldn't be here."

There was a dim echo of automatic fire, which ended abruptly.

Rahel tapped the earpiece. "The radio's not working. Who's doing this? Why are they here for you?"

Lukas frowned. "That's a good question. And it's only one person."

"One person can't get into this place."

"He's already in."

Rahel was uncertain about what to do, torn between heading out to find out what was going on and remaining with the only person who had some idea of what was going on.

"Are you armed?" Lukas asked her.

"No. We can't be armed around a prisoner."

"Prudent," Lukas said.

There were several more bursts of weapons' firing.

"I should go—" Rahel began after a couple of minutes of silence.

"I wouldn't," Lukas said. He looked past her to the heavy metal door. "He's here."

The door swung open and Legion entered, both daggers sheathed. He paused, taking in Lukas and Rahel. "Do you know where she is?" he asked Lukas.

Lukas indicated Rahel. "She does. The file."

Legion strode toward her, drawing one dagger but stopped abruptly as an old woman with a leather-bound book in the crook of her arm stepped out of the shadows, materializing as if she'd never been there but always been there. She was draped in a black robe with a black hood placing her face in shadow.

"Why do you interfere, old woman?" Legion demanded.

"We never interfere," she said.

"Your sister interfered recently," Legion said. "I was close to *her*," he added to Lukas. "But not in this timeline."

"I am not here to interfere," the old woman said.

Rahel took a step closer to Lukas. "Who are you?" The question was directed at both Legion and the old woman.

Lukas pointed at the woman first. "That is Clotho. She spins the thread of life." He indicated the man. "That is one of *We*. Legion."

Rahel turned toward him. "'*We*'?"

Lukas plucked the file folder from her hand. "Thank you for finding her."

Rahel staggered back, the gurney keeping her from falling over. "All this to get us to find her for you?"

Lukas held out the file and Legion took it from him "Yes. As you noted. Your people are the best in this timeline."

"Who are you?" Rahel asked. "How can you have the same DNA as her? Who is she? Why is she so important?"

Legion opened the folder, but glanced at Clotho first, as if concerned she would stop him, despite her words. She remained still, peering out from under her black hood. He read while Lukas reached out and placed his hands on Rahel's shoulders. "I told you to leave."

But he abruptly let go of her as Clotho walked, more glided, forward.

"She is mine," Clotho said.

Lukas shrugged. "She's not important any more. We have what we wanted." He looked at Legion. "Do you know where?"

"Yes," Legion said.

Rahel interrupted them as Clotho reached for her. "Why?"

Clotho's hand paused, inches from Rahel.

Lukas blinked, as if the question confused him. "'Why'? It is what I must do."

"You're going to kill her?" Rahel asked.

Lukas shook his head. "No. She is also part of *We*. We'd hoped she is the completion of *We*."

"We must go," Legion said, moving toward the door. "Reinforcements are on the way. We have what we need."

Lukas looked at Rahel. "You should never have come to this place." He headed for the door.

"Legion," Rahel said, causing both men to pause. They turned toward her as she continued. "When Jesus encountered a possessed man, he called on the demons to emerge. When they did, he demanded their name. The demons replied 'we are Legion'. And they were afraid he would cast them into the abyss so they begged him for mercy. I think you've been here before. In the desert. And you begged for mercy. Like cowards."

Legion and Lukas exchanged a glance.

"Do you know what happened to the demons?" Rahel demanded, taking a step toward them, past Clotho. "He sent them into a herd of pigs. Who then rushed into a lake and drowned."

Lukas shook his head. "I am sorry about your husband and son. You should not have come to a place like this." He strode out the door behind Legion.

As they exited the room, Lukas and Legion snapped out of this plane of existence.

Cloth put her hands on Rahel. "Be at peace. It is your time to join your family."

Lara

I WAS SO SOUND ASLEEP THAT it took Seth a long time of knocking to wake me up. I'm starting to wonder if I sleep at all? Don't you go psychotic if you didn't get enough sleep? I somehow seem to think you did. Can I go more psychotic if I'm already psychotic? Is it a finite thing or just different shades till you're way down the rabbit hole playing with your own poop? I'm starting not to care and it's odd but the Fourth Floor is beginning to feel like coming home.

"Come in," I call out, and that's when it occurs to me to wonder how I know it's Seth on the other side of the door.

Seth's voice echoes through the thick steel. "Can't. You're locked in."

Why am I locked in while Mr. Hammer gets to wander about? "Can't open from this side." I look through the tiny window, wishing Seth wasn't so cute.

"Uhhh, you manipulated Claude into killing Sam?" he asks.

"Claude killed Sam?" I say, trying to process this revelation.

"Yeah, how'd you do that? I can't even manipulate him into a game of checkers."

I start to feel bad for Claude. "Really, he killed Sam? How'd he do it?"

"Choked him with his cuffs," Seth says, then adds, "Hey, that's almost a mercy killing for someone like Claude. How'd you do it?"

"I didn't do anything," I protest. *Right*? Or had I?

"We got a new guard though," Seth says. "She's pretty nice."

"She?" I ask and as if by magic, I see some blond hair a bit lower than Seth's face and hear the bolt sliding.

"Looks like you're getting out," Seth sorta yells through the glass and the door opens and there stands Jess, same washed out blue eyes and same dour look. I know she belongs here somehow but not as Sam's replacement.

Her nametag reads Julia Stone. I'm beginning to see that while the faces stay the same that the personalities change, as do the names, yet the first letters seem to stay constant; maybe it's some alliterative device to help me remember. Geez, alliterative? At this moment, I'd give a huge fucking chunk of my vocabulary to remember one real thing about myself.

Julia Stone eyes me. "You've got to meet the doctor. Then lunch. Give me any lip and no lunch for you."

She's coming on strong, maybe to get hand over me. As if having the key cards isn't enough?

No lunch is fine with me cause I can still taste the cookie, but my back doesn't hurt and I glance down at my fingers and there isn't a blister to be seen. Maybe wherever my head went my stomach followed but the rest of me stayed put? You can only stay in the moment for so long, I think and I'm really getting sick of this.

"Which doctor?" I ask and Seth grabs my arm as if I'm on dangerous ground and he's pulling me to safety, which is a bit disconcerting coming from a guy capable of what he's capable of.

"There's only one doctor up here," she says.

"Lily," Seth says, trying to warn me about something. Like things can get worse?

Julia leads me down a hallway, a long white one, and I notice there's a pay phone at the end of it and I've been here before, except not really here. And why do they have a pay phone in a lock down, except maybe it's a trap? Maybe it only dials one number? Maybe the CIA has it tapped and I know I'm sliding into Claude territory and that's not good, especially since he just killed Sam-I-Am.

But before I can dwell too long on that, Julia raps her knuckles on a thin door.

A voice comes from within: "Yes?"

Julia cracks open the door. "Doctor Jenkins? Lily Cole."

Julia half-shoves me into the office. Jenkins is sitting there; a thick file on the desk in front of her, reading glasses perched on her nose.

She smiles, but not a happy smile, some other kind of smile. "I'm glad you're here, Lily. I was just reading your file. Perhaps you can clear some things up for me."

I'm kinda hoping the opposite, but I'm in too deep now.

Jenkins waves me to a seat. "You can go, Julia."

What is with these docs, dismissing their protection like so much kitchen help? Of course, it appears Sam-I-Am couldn't even protect himself.

The door shuts as I sit down. A hard plastic seat, not exactly something to make me comfortable enough to spill my guts, rather my brain, but I don't really have access too much up there anyway.

I am interested in the file, though. There's my life, I guess, all clipped together so neatly. I'd really like to know what's there. Perhaps she'll let me read it?

I don't think so.

Before Jenkins can try to drill into my brain for what I don't know, her phone rings. She answers, but I'm more focused on the file, trying to read upside down, which is harder that you'd think it is.

Wichita. Really?

I don't think so.

But this reminds me of something and I feel a little sick to my stomach, and not just from the other lunch.

I lean forward, trying to read more, but Jenkins puts the phone down with more force than is necessary. "Lily."

"Yes?"

She shuts the folder. "How did you know my name?"

"I read it on you jacket."

"Don't lie," Jenkins says, in a not-so-comforting-therapy-voice, but more a no-bullshit-not-so-therapy-voice.

"It was—"

"Lily." She gets up and walks over to the white coat hanging on the rack. Grabs it, Tugs it on, then presents it to me. There's no name sewn above the left pocket. "Try again, Lily."

"I don't know."

I'd seen it. Of course, I'd seen her before I'd seen it and now I'm looping into whatever and I feel my hands start to shake.

Jenkins sits down. She pulls open a drawer. I hear a crinkle of plastic, which reminded me of…

She puts a Ziploc bag on her desk, a wad of papers stuffed inside. "What's this?"

She has my memory. Fuck me. She knows I escaped. She knows I can edge.

She pulls open the zip on the Ziploc. Unfolds the papers. I strain to see what's on them, because I know they're my memories but I don't remember my memories, so I want to know.

She makes it easy, holding them up. "What is this?" she asks again.

It's not writing. It's drawing. Or something. I have no idea what it is, so I don't answer, but I'm depressed because whatever memories I might have had of my escape are gibberish; if that's what this is.

"It was in your jeans," Jenkins says.

94

I guess that means I own it. "Just some stuff." But as I look at it, the drawings transform themselves into something I recognize, that I can understand.

Before there was just me now, there was a bunch of other stuff that I don't remember. People keep telling me I should remember, but maybe if you can't remember there's a reason.

She puts it down on her desk before I can read any further.

"It looks like some form of code," Jenkins says. "Yet it also looks old. Like Egyptian hieroglyphics. We've got people analyzing it."

My people should meet your people, I think and I giggle.

"What's so funny?" Jenkins demands. She leans forward to indicate her seriousness. "This is the Fourth Floor, Lily. You're in a very different world now."

I know better, but I can't stop another giggle. A different world? Like what else is new? I also know I'm unraveling, I can feel it.

"We look for people like you, Lily. People who are different. We want to understand you. How your brain works."

I think of the whack jobs in the cafeteria. Apparently different means nut-job killers, which depresses me because it means maybe I really did kill my family.

"It takes a while to get up here," Jenkins continued. "You bounced up to the second and third floor several times to get examined."

That isn't good news. I have no memory of a second and third floor. Not even a dream or nightmare.

"How does you head feel?" Jenkins asks, out of nowhere.

"Okay?"

"The incisions? They appear to be healing nicely."

"The staples?"

Jenkins looks at me with a sad smile and she doesn't seem the sort. So I know it's really bad. She reaches into a drawer and retrieves a mirror, one of those things they hold up in a salon so you can see the back of your head.

She gets up, sticks it in front of me. My skull is shaved, not a hint of hair. Savage red scars crisscross my noggin. She starts to move it so I can see the side and back, but really, could it get better?

* * *

I walk down to the cafeteria with Julia and all my swell friends are there. I want to skip lunch but watch as Seth fills up his plate with the linguine. He seems awfully slim for someone who eats so many carbs and I decide that Martha wouldn't be pleased with him. Which is an odd thing to think as I see Maria sitting there eating another hot dog. There's a symbolism here that I decide to ignore. Jim calls me over and he seems happier than most to see me.

"So, Lily, that was pretty good work, the way you got Claude to do that. Sam was a sadist shithead," says the Footlocker Man.

"I didn't make him do a thing. I wanted to kill Sam myself. But Claude said you all had a pact about him cause he only took one taste."

Maria puts down the hotdog and asks, "Who told you he only took one taste?"

"Claude did. Said that's why he was okay, cause then he'd leave you alone."

The three psychopaths laugh, which is not nearly as pleasant as the weeders when they laughed.

Jim says, "You're sorta naive Lily Squared. I guess its cause you're so young."

I feel a chill run down my spine at the thought of Sam coming back into my cell. Now I'm very happy he's dead even though I feel bad about Claude.

Maria stares at me. "He was awful, just awful, but none of us wanted to risk getting the death penalty."

"What?" I ask. "But, he's already here. Insane. He can't get the death penalty."

Seth shakes his head. "Just insane for what we did before, but not whether it's legally insane or not what we do here. If they decide he's legally sane now, killing Sam, then he goes to death row, which most of us would be on except the law previously decided we're legally insane."

This isn't making any sense to me.

Maria nods. "Yeah, that's why none of us would bother with Sam cause it's a pretty normal thing to kill him and then you'd be legally sane doing that and they can fry you."

"Inject you," Jim says.

Yeah, this conversation sucks. "But, I haven't even been to court," I say. "Why am I here?"

Seth squints. "But you have been to court, Lily. I get twenty minutes of supervised computer time in the library every week and I Googled you."

"There's a library?" I ask.

"I really liked your Facebook page," Seth adds.

I'm still processing. "A trial? There was a trial?"

"Yeah," Seth says.

"When do I get my computer time cause I'd very much like to Google myself?"

Maria shakes her head. "It's a privilege and you get points and I've been here four years and don't have enough."

Jim grins. "Cause you fight too much."

"Only with you, asshole," she says and grabs that hot dog bun again.

Jim says, "You can't watch porn, it's supervised."

I want to say that you, Jim, got all the porn you need in your head but I don't cause I'm thinking about a trial I don't remember and that was sorta a while ago and now I'm here? That makes enough sense for me to realize that any day I might suddenly remember killing a whole family, which I'd forgotten. I feel a bit sick.

Suddenly the double doors swing open and Claude, followed by a stern Julia, walks in and everyone cheers. I don't cheer cause I suddenly realize why he did it. He'd wanted to kill Sam all along but didn't want to fry or get injected for it so he'd used me by proxy. That makes me the evilest person in this room. I'm Charlie Manson bad, capable of making even a stone cold killer, kill just for me. Fuck and I'd just won a cookie for most weeds; really do those two things go together?

I don't think so.

I'm sorta sick of living in the moment cause so far it hasn't gotten me much.

"Claude doesn't think I killed my family," I say and they all glance at me for a moment until I realize what I'd said.

Claude had killed a man somewhere between my being lost in a forest and winning a cookie and I was using him as my moral proof of my basic decency. They all get points for letting that comment slide. Claude sits down with a flourish reserved for Nobel Prize winners or some neurosurgeon who'd just clipped off a huge aneurism.

Exhausting. How did I learn so much crap about the world in sixteen years or maybe more? I must have been reading all the time. When did I even have the time to be around people long enough to need to kill them? Was I sitting there memorizing Wikipedia and someone bothered me and I waited till they were all asleep and stabbed them to death cause you know conglomerations are so fascinating?

Claude is beaming at me. Actually, it isn't a bad look on him. Better than the dead eyes above me when I woke to his raping me in his truck. But this isn't that guy, right? That was Sam-I-Am? Wait. Jake in the truck; the first Jake. I'm guessing here.

"Claude, did I make you get rid of Sam?" I ask.

"Nah. No one *makes* me do nothing. But I really *did* do it for you; it's like the most normal thing I've done here and I feel pretty good. I think my therapy is paying off."

"Really?" I say. "You get therapy?"

"Plus," Claude drops his voice to a whisper, "she said it was Sam's time."

"'She'?" I ask.

"The old lady," Claude says.

"You saw her?" Jim asks.

Before I can delve into that, Maria has that last bite of hotdog, the one that makes her almost choke and then says, "Lily Squared here says you told her that you didn't think she killed her family."

Claude grins. "Yeah, I was trying out the lie seeing if it would fly," and they all say oh, like it's the most understandable thing in the world.

Seth sees my confusion and says, "Yeah, you're still a bit catatonic aren't you? Not quite all here?"

Ya think? I want to scream but I have to live in the moment and fuck me this is a hard moment to live in. Seth is sucking up a linguini and half of it is still dangling like a worm that sorta knows it's on a hook but hasn't quite accepted the reality of that. He says, "Claude was practicing the lie."

I say, "On me."

And he says, "No, on himself," and they all nod. Seth continues. "Yeah, if we can believe the lie, than anyone will. Because if you believe the lie, then it's not a lie. Really like if the president does it, it's not illegal. Come on Lily Squared."

And hearing that name from Seth made me rather sad, sadder than I already was.

Seth leans close. "If I really believe the lie than anyone else will. It's like: *Laura, baby, I do love you and yeah, I miss you and I know we're broke up but just meet me after work and let me kiss you one last time so we can go forth and love again?*"

I feel a chill. "Laura. Was that your girlfriend? The one you beat to death with a hammer behind Denny's after her shift?"

"Yeah, and she was afraid of me as she should have been, but how else could I have gotten her to trust me enough so I could kill her?"

I'm sweating this lunch which has turned into one big way too much information fuck fest and I really want to go back to sleep and get lost in the woods or maybe get raped by Sam-I-Am again, except he was dead, so then maybe Jake, the first Jake. I don't care much at this point.

Maria says, "*Hey, let's play gin rummy and I'll let you win and here have a beer so I can blow your cheating head off.*"

Jim says, "I knew it was the cheating," and adds, "*Yes, my dear, you can make those points up with some extra credit work meet me at 10 by the student center and I'll drive you home.*"

"You were a professor," I say.

"Course I was. How else do you meet college students?"

And I say, focusing on the singular: "Student. How would you meet a student? I thought maybe you were a janitor or fireman or something. What did you teach?"

"Systems Engineering. A very logical thing which few are really good at and I was very good at it."

"Well, you got caught," I say.

He smiles. "Once. I got caught *once* because for everyone like us, texting is just the bane of our lives. We shouldn't do it. I'd been working on an app that wipes out all traces of a text ten seconds after clicked on. But I got caught before I could finish it. Shoulda waited."

"How come no one said anything about my head?" I ask.

They exchange confused looks.

"You have a mirror in your cell," Jim says.

"We're polite here," Seth adds. "No sense talking about the obvious."

"The hair will grow back," Maria adds, though not helpful.

"When did the cuts happen?"

Claude shakes his head. "Second and third floor, Lily. You don't remember that either?"

"That's a good thing," Jim says. "Not remembering those floors." He reaches up and parts his hair so I can see a scar running front to rear in the center of his scalp.

Maria leans forward and taps the base of her skull while lifting her hair. "It hurt for a long time. Does your hurt?"

"No," I say, supposing I should be grateful for the little things in life. But then I see her. Sally. She with the silver streak in her hair, except now its been let free, long and flowing, not tied up. She walks in and sits next to Jim without even a how-do-you-do to me as if she doesn't recognize me. How could you not, with this head? I'm trying to remember if I looked in the mirror at Martha's place.

I did, I know I did. I had hair. I used that brush.

And Jim says, "hello," as if he knows her.

She replies, "hello, Jim."

I say, "hello, Sally," and you think I'd have learned my lesson as she turns to me. "It's Sarah, honey." But then she smiles, a genuine smile, just like the Sally I knew, know, imagined?

Footlocker Jim suddenly becomes a completely different man who you'd never guess had ever been called Footlocker Jim and says, "This is my dear friend, Sarah. She's quite brilliant. Even more than I. We taught at the same college. Sarah has a doctorate in Theoretical Physics. And one in mythology."

Those don't seem to jive to me. And suddenly all the nuts stand up, except for me and her, and walk away. Just before he leaves, Claude leans over and whispers in my ear—"You didn't kill your family. You just need to keep up the lie here. Sarah is gonna help you because you helped me."

And then he's off and I'm looking at Sarah's kind face and for just a moment, I feel at peace. But then I'm leery. Who to believe? Claude? Who killed Sam-I-Am. Sarah/Sally? Doctor Jenkins? No one?

"So, who did you kill?" I say as a conversation starter, staying on a safe topic of conversation on the Fourth Floor.

She's picking at a salad with much less gusto than I've seen her eat a chicken salad sandwich. Her hair is amazing and I can't help stare at it.

"In this reality I killed my lab assistant," she says and takes a bite of salad. "Except she wasn't exactly a lab assistant. She was Joan. Martha's assistant. And she would have killed me. But I got her first. We have to be careful. They're everywhere."

I start to get up cause thank-you-Claude but this is not the help I need.

She grabs my wrist and she has a firm grip and I think its cause she's done a lot of weeding.

"I need to go lie down," I say with such ferocity that she does let go and she says, "I'll be here, there, when you wake up."

* * *

Lara had decided as soon as she met Sarah, or whatever her name was, that she wanted to go back to the tulips. It wasn't much to ask she thought and after that, lunch of crazy topped with crazy all she wanted was the methodical losing yourself in pulling weeds.

Julia escorted her to her cell and she heard the bolt click and she curled back into the ball of what she hoped was a better place and covered her head and prayed for sleep. When it came it was not what she'd hoped it would be.

Of course it wasn't.

She turned over on the mattress and instead of a cement block wall painted a sickly gray she saw wallpaper of tangled Ivy leaves. She looked around the room and there were pictures everywhere of the girl from the Facebook page. There was a small desk and a laptop. A bookshelf full of books and too many stuffed animals to count and then she saw the cat. The one so well stroked from the first floor. One glass eye was missing and Lara jumped out of bed and grabbed it and as she did that she thought-- these are nice sheets. Soft, smooth, a high thread count. She sat in the corner and stroked the cat until there was a knock on the door. Her life seemed to be a series of knocked upon doors. *Lara?* She heard a woman say, *"Lara, time to get dressed. Big day at school you know?"*

No, she didn't know, but live in the moment, she thought.

100

She went to the closet and there was that ironed calico shirt and the terrible jeans, but she put them on because this was the moment and Lara knew she had to see how it played out. She dressed and washed her face and made her bed and brushed her teeth for two minutes like a good girl should. She walked over to the laptop and opened it and found her Facebook page, the one named Lily Cole because that's how she hid it from her father by calling it Lily Cole instead of Lara Coleman. There were several likes about her butt selfie and she felt a moment's pride before she closed it knowing that no one would ever update it again. She walked down the stairs and Martha and Jake were sitting at the kitchen table. Or was it Maria and Jim? Lara was no longer sure about anything except she wished she'd stayed with Sarah because she didn't want to be here. She knew with all her heart that she did not want to be here. She wanted to be pulling weeds out of the tulips. It seemed like such a small thing to want.

Lara sat down in front of a bowl of oatmeal knowing it was hers. The man she knew as Jake or Jim looked over at the woman she knew as Martha or Maria and said, *"Mary, I need some butter. Goddamn your worthless self. When will you ever do one thing right?"*

Mary jumped up like a woman very used to jumping up and said, *"I'm sorry, John. I don't know why I forget these things I'm so stupid sometimes* and he nodded and said *yeah, I don't know why I put up with you."*

Lara wanted to wake up. Lara was done here in this place so horrible that she wiped it clean away. A boy and girl walked down the stairs and joined them and Mary gave them each a plate of toast and scrambled eggs and Lara was so happy that she'd never seen them before. They were no part of this game playing over and over in Lara's head and she found them tragic, and innocent and young.

John looked at the young boy and said, *"George, five PM, me and you and that punching bag in the basement. You can't keep letting those boys on the bus disrespect you like they do. You have to fight back. You'll never be a man until you know what it means to defend yourself and this family from all the little shits trying to disrespect us. When you let those little shits humiliate you, they are humiliating your family and me because you are my son. You're are a part of me out there representing this family and I will not allow you to tear down what I've built up because you're scared."*

George said, *"I'm not scared dad, I just don't want to hit them."*

John slapped him so hard that his head hit the wall directly behind his chair and Mary said, *"Listen to your father. He knows what's best"*, but her tone was so tight and frightened that Lara wanted to grab her head and shake it till Mary grew an inch of backbone.

"You study for that spelling test, Sarah?" John asked the young girl sitting next to Lara.

"Yes, daddy, all the time before lights out. I studied good daddy."

John leaned back and his chair creaked a bit and said, *"Spell conglomerate."*

Sarah was silent for a moment and said, *"I can write it, Daddy. I can, but it's harder out loud. But the test is going to be all written so I will do good, daddy, I will."*

And John tipped his chair forward and said, *Spell conglomerate* and Sarah said, *C O N,* and her voice was full of fear and Lara stood up and said, *"Who the hell do you think you are?"* She stood up so quickly that her chair fell over with a loud thud and Mary and George and Sarah froze. They all shrank into such smaller versions of themselves that Lara could almost see them disappear.

Lara wanted to kill him, to chop him up into tiny pieces and stuff him in a footlocker and she was thinking that when the plate flew across the table and hit her squarely in the face. She almost fainted from the pain. She almost fainted from the sound of her nose breaking under the combined physics of the velocity of the plate and the force behind the throw. But, she didn't. She stood and held onto the table and watched his face turn into a smile. A smile she knew, a smile she'd seen so many times before and she said, *"You can't hurt me anymore."*

He looked at his watch and said, *"I have a meeting"*, and walked out like he owned the world because Lara finally got it: he did own the world.

Mary grabbed her and took her to the sink and bent her over backwards till she thought her spine would break and ran cold water on her face. And Lara could feel the blood running down her throat faster than it could escape her swelling nostrils.

Mary said, *"There, there, why do you do this? You know what he's like why do you provoke him?"*

And Lara said, *"Because you won't. Because someone has to change things,"* and she started to choke on her own blood and then she passed out.

The Institution

"If your mind carries a heavy burden of past, you will experience more of the same. The past perpetuates itself through lack of presence. The quality of your consciousness at this moment is what shapes the future." Eckhart Tolle

JACOBSON SPUN THE combination on the cheap office safe, unaware of the irony that it was set to his ex-wife's birth date. He pulled the copy of Lily Cole's file out. Put it on his desk. Just as he was about to settle his weight down in the chair, he abruptly hustled over to the door and turned the lock. He went back and down, chair springs protesting.

He pondered what sort of woman could compel a man like Claude to do what he'd done? Sam had been a guard for eighteen years before he took Lily and put her on the Fourth Floor. At least that's what Mary-Louise had told him in between hysterical sobs.

There was nothing as evil as an evil woman, Jacobson thought as he flipped the file open and began to read. He'd only glanced at it during intake, enough to gather the pertinent data: Lily Cole had been found guilty of killing her mother, father, brother and sister. It was only after this, during sentencing, that the court appointed psychiatrist had recommended she be remanded to the Institution rather than the general prison population.

Jacobson was surprised to see that the finding had been what he'd considered his original one: Transient Global Amnesia. Jacobson tried to remember back, but those first months here were a blur, obscured by a lot of alcohol and pills. Had he been that screwed up that he'd simply rubber-stamped some court-appointed hack?

Which did make him realize he was at that same level, sitting here in his locked office in the Institution with barred windows. A hack for the state, or whoever ran this place, hitting rock bottom for his profession, pushing cases through and not giving a shit.

Which reminded him—who the hell did they work for if they didn't work for the state? And how much more was Jenkins getting paid?

Jacobson flipped pages. He found the section on the trial and was surprised, given that the psychiatrist had so easily gotten her remanded here, that her lawyer hadn't tried for an insanity defense. Granted such a defense was a long shot, but as Jenkins had noted, the police had a rock solid case against Lily: knife in hand, no one else in house, her younger brother dying as they entered.

Jacobson frowned.

She'd pled not guilty.

The court-appointed defense lawyer had done the best he could. Claimed that Lily had been defending her family against an attacker. One who the security cameras on the outside of the house didn't record. Whom crime scene investigation found no trace of.

There was only Lily Cole with a knife, in the kitchen, with the bodies of her family scattered about the house.

Jacobson re-read the material, the mind that had blazed in medical school finally beginning to churn.

Something was wrong about all this.

The head wound? Jacobson frowned. The police and prosecutor put if off to her own father trying to stop her, before she killed him by slitting his throat.

Except they never produced what had caused the head wound.

Just as the defense attorney couldn't produce another person at the scene. He said she sustained it defending her family against this invisible attacker.

He opened her file to the pictures the police had taken after Lily's rampage. Her father, John, lying on his back in bed, stabbed so many times that the flowered comforter over him was nothing but red and not red but more black. His wife, Mary, on the bathroom floor where she'd tried to run. She'd locked the bathroom door against her own daughter wielding the knife with such fury that she's kicked the door completely off the hinges. Mary was killed with a knife so long it had severed her spine. Jacobson shook his head. She'd known in her last moments that the hand that was killing her was the grown hand of the daughter she'd once held at her breast, nursed and loved and cared for but she had no idea she was nursing a viper.

No one sees the viper till it strikes Jacobson thought as he pulled a power bar out the drawer, inherently believing it was better than candy because of the title. He wolfed it down in a couple of bites, while staring at pictures of a massacre. He was satiated for just a while until the raging hunger struck him again, the hunger he thought was real and for food but it was for vengeance. Jacobson imagined Lily feeling so sure of herself that she could doze on the Fourth Floor where no one was her match. Poor

Sam who had to die because he was just another limping gazelle in the face of the pure evil that was Lily Cole.

Poor, dumb Claude who was merely the hyena to Lily's lion. Chewing off the remnants of whatever she'd walk away and leave him. He felt sick and then he turned to the pictures of the girl. Sarah. A tiny bundle of hair poking out of a blood-soaked comforter.

Jacobson could feel his heart thumping in his chest, his anger raising his blood pressure and his pulse. He looked at the last photos of young George who'd crawled so deep into his own closet that Lily's knife had gouged the drywall more than it had struck him.

The only positive was that Lily had managed to strike his main aorta and he'd died quickly and for that Dr. Jacobson was grateful. He opened the drawer on the left and reached for one of the pill bottles in the middle of others. He shook out four one mg Xanax and swallowed them with a swag of cold coffee.

He sat there for twenty minutes until the pills did what they did and slowed his heartbeat and he knew with all his heart that Jeannie would pay for what she'd done to him. Lily Cole had finally done what nothing else had: he would have payback against the snakes. He'd become the man he once was and he'd take care of Jeannie. He felt calm; his chest was no longer so tight like an elephant was standing on it. He was the elephant. He was the elephant who would stomp Jeannie flat.

Then his door imploded and someone much worse than a snake in human skin entered.

LARA

"There is no coming to consciousness without pain. People will do anything, no matter how absurd, in order to avoid facing their own Soul. One does not become enlightened by imagining figures of light, but by making the darkness conscious." Jung

I wake up to not so gentle nudges in my ribs. I see the rubber boots and don't even have to look up to know who is kicking me.

What the hell are you doing? Joan says in a voice actually filled with wonder cause she really can't even imagine what I'm doing, sleeping instead of working. *Do you think Martha pays you to sleep?*

I stand up and brush the mulch off me but it doesn't brush away, it just smears onto my clothes. I touch my face, my nose, which both seem to be fine but I know so much more now and frankly, I'm rather sick of Joan.

I stand as tall as I can and I'm still at her collarbones. *No. I do not think Martha pays me to sleep. I think she buys one extra cookie to make hard labor more palatable to the people who have no other choice. I think she thinks she's God and you are her faithful Peter out here building a church for her, when in reality she could give a shit about you. You can make this place so perfect that no weed could grow here for years cause there's not one single root left and she still won't give a flying fuck about you because she can't. Do you get that—she can't? She's not exactly like Claude or Maria but worse. You could burst into spontaneous flames and Martha wouldn't pick up a hose to douse you down.*

Joan takes a step back. *Who's Claude, who's Maria?*

Nobodies, I scream. *They're nobodies like you are, but they got the fucking sense to not care about anyone at all. They're luckier than you, who thinks you might get a bone if you just work hard enough and, most importantly, follow the damn rules. Always the rules. And following the rules? No!*

I see a tear start to run down her leathered skin and I feel bad about that cause Martha would never shed a tear for her. Joan's a good woman who just forgot that she's a person too. She turns away and says, *Martha wants you for dinner,* and I can tell how much even saying that hurt her.

I wonder how many buckets she's emptied for someone who'd never think to invite her for dinner and I suspect it's been a lot.

Go shower, there are clothes in the bathroom. Go clean yourself up. They're waiting for you. And she starts to march away like the good Praetorian Guard that she is. I grab her and I hug her; my mulch covered body flaking off onto her own and stand on tippy toes in my boots and whisper as close as I can get to her ear, *You're a good woman Joan. You don't have to be her lapdog. She's just a human being like you are. Don't give her your life thinking you'll get something back. You never will.*

And she shoves me away because I'd said too much.

I lift the rabbit and take the key and get cleaned up. I walk down the trail and skip the front door and go into the open garage door. Jake is in the bed of the truck and he's leaning over the opened footlocker and I can see that there's nothing there to do with fighting a fire in there. He slams the lid and says, *Oh, I didn't hear you.*

I say, *You can't do it Jake,* and he says, *What?*

Whatever you have in that footlocker that you think will set you free."

Jake says, *Nothing there but boots and coats,* and I say, *Do I look that stupid to you? Why do you think she invited me for dinner?*

And he says, *Frankly, I don't know. I don't know why she picked you up off the street or brought you here in the first place or let you come back. None of that is like her.*

I agree. *No, none of it is like her but you need to ask yourself why?* I point to the footlocker. *"None of that is you, it's not who you are and you'll never be able to do it. You think it's the thing that makes all this livable but it only makes it sufferable.*

I lean against the truck in the perfect garage, which had been my safe place and look up at him. *You need to get in this truck and drive away because the only thing keeping you here is your own idea that it might be different one day if you do it all just right. But, there is no right. There's nothing for you here. If you leave now, you may catch Joan.*

And I turn and walk out toward the path and he says, *Aren't you coming for dinner?*

I say, *No. There is nothing for me here. I just know that.*

And I walk back, lift the rabbit and take the key. I go and fall onto the perfect white couch cushions that had so absorbed Joan. Right before I fall asleep, I hear truck wheels on a gravel road and I go to sleep for the very first time with a smile on my face.

* * *

Lara wakes and sees the concrete blocks and feels one second of reassurance and then a hand clamps over her mouth. A body much larger than her own flips her over and she feels a heavy arm across her neck. She can see the door to her cell is open but it's dark. So dark that there are no mealtimes. Just this arm choking the breath out of her and this weight ten times worse than Sam because some part of her had known Sam wanted a taste. But this isn't a taste, this is an envelopment, a devouring, a being smashed out of existence and she tries to say please, but nothing comes out because no air is going out.

She's starting to faint and suddenly she's in the room with the ivy wall papered walls and she hears a terrible noise and jumps up and runs into the hall and she sees Seth and he says, *I'm setting you free Laura. I'm setting you all free* and she says *No, please, no* and he says *you have two black eyes, Laura. I love you and you matter to me and I'm not gonna let all this happen.*

She grabs him and can see the glint of the hammer in his hand and she says, *You're not doing it for me. You're doing it for yourself because you like it. You're going to like this and then you're going to kill a girl with a hammer because you just like it. It makes you feel powerful. Please, please don't.*

He grabs Lara and slams her head into the ivy colored wall and says, *Who do you think you are? You don't get to tell me what to do,* and then he's gone and Lara fades away and wakes to the kitchen, the one she doesn't want to be in and the knife is in her hand.

She looks at the blood trail leading to the door. To where she doesn't want to go, but she goes, she walks to the door and shoves it open to a dark room.

A man stands in there; a knife in his hand, blood dripping from the blade and Lara knows it's too late. The man steps toward her, into the light from the kitchen behind her, and she recognizes him, but it takes a moment for the recognition to retrieve the exact moment.

It says the name right there on his blue shirt. Joey. From the diner in Boise.

You Okay?

She knows with all her heart that she didn't stab anyone fifty-four times. Especially not her little brother.

He's moving smooth, so smoothly, closing the distance between the two of them, without seeming to. It's like she was the only person in the universe to him.

A girl like you shouldn't be all alone, he says.

But I'm not alone, Lara says.

He stops. Raises an eyebrow, looks past her into the kitchen, then focuses back on Lara. *I don't see anyone else.*

Lara smiles. *I'm Lara. I'm Lily. I'm a lot of people.*

Okey-dokey. He raises the knife to the ready position. "*You want some pie?*

Sure.

This gives Joey pause. He moves to his left, but Lara doesn't react, the knife dangling at her side. She's done, worn out, tired of all the times and places and games and people.

Are you going to try to defend yourself? Joey asks.

Why? I know it wasn't me. I didn't kill them. You did.

I did in this timeline," Joey says. "*Who knows what you did in other timelines? And your boyfriend, Seth? Who knows?*

Then he attacks.

The Institution

"The ordinary response to atrocities is to banish them from consciousness." Judith Lewis Herman, **Trauma and Recovery: The Aftermath of Violence**

"WHERE IS SHE?" Legion demanded, a single dagger drawn.

Dr. Jacobson was too shocked to respond. He shoved his chair back from his desk, but the wheels, bogged down by his weight, only moved a few inches.

Lukas walked around the desk. "Lily Cole. Where is she?" He leaned forward and slapped Jacobson across the face.

"Who are you?" Jacobson sputtered, one hand reaching for the red alert button underneath the top of the desk.

Lukas neatly sliced that hand off with one swipe of the second dagger, which Legion had given him.

Jacobson didn't react for a moment, staring at the hand tumbling to the floor, then the spurt of blood from the stump.

Then he screamed.

Lukas and Legion exchanged disgusted glances, barely more than a twinge of emotion most people wouldn't have caught. Jacobson fell of his chair to the floor, curled up, cradling his arm. Even though he was a trained physician, he wasn't taking the proper action to stop the bleeding.

Lukas ignored him, looking at the folder open on the desk. The transfer order was off to one side. "She's been moved to the fourth floor," he said. But he also saw the crime scene photos, spread out, and an orgy of blood. "Did we do this?" he asked.

Legion walked to the front of the desk and glanced down. "Does it matter?"

Lukas looked up. "I can't remember much. Why would we do this?"

"Help me," Jacobson whined from the floor.

"Come, brother," Legion said, indicating the door.

"Help me," Jacobson repeated.

Lukas was still staring at the photos, frowning, trying to remember what he couldn't remember.

Legion walked around the desk, put a foot on Jacobson's shoulder, and shoved him over so that he was facing up. Then quickly sliced the doctor's throat.

"Let's go." A woman stood in the doorway. Martha, but not Martha, dressed in a medium length green tunic and black hunting boots. She had a short bow in hand, a quiver over one shoulder.

Jacobson's last thought was of that bottle of Xanax in Jeannie's medicine cabinet.

Lara

"Properly speaking, the unconscious is the real psychic; its inner nature is just as unknown to us as the reality of the external world, and it is just as imperfectly reported to us through the data of consciousness as is the external world through the indications of our sensory organs." Sigmund Freud. **The Interpretation of Dreams**

I WAKE UP. I CAN'T BREATHE. I'm choking. I begin to panic, but instead of the weight on top of me or the blade across my throat, there are just things, light things, tubes and IV lines. I try to rip them out. I'm fighting to breathe. I'm so tired, so very tired and suddenly Joan is there above me, as tall and regal as ever and she's saying, *Relax, relax, Lara.* She's stoking my arm and I try to relax. But she's dressed in scrubs and has a stethoscope around her neck, which makes me wonder how the weeds are doing.

I try to live in the moment and she says, *The doctor will be here in a few seconds. Really, he will be, just trust me and let the tube breath for you,* and I think, *what tube?* Where am I? This is worse than lost in the forest. This is the worst waking ever and I clutch her arm so hard that my nails leave a mark because I'm suffocating here and then Dr. Jacobson is above me but he's not fat.

I'm so very tired. So sick of it all. I want to die and I tried with Joey. But, I can't. I feel the tube being pulled from my throat and it hurts and I open my eyes to the same bright room but there are machines everywhere and hisses and pumps and people all around me and I feel the tape on my throat. I see Jake/Jim/John and he leans over me and kisses my forehead and says, *Oh, my darling daughter we never thought you'd come back to us.*

The room is filled with sunshine and the slim Dr. Jacobson is standing behind Martha/Maria/Mary like he just delivered a healthy eight-pound girl. And maybe he did. I pass in and out of consciousness and keep coming back here. Little Sarah is reading me 'Green Eggs and Ham' and even smaller George keeps changing his iPhone from Johnny Cash to Lucinda Williams.

I can't stay awake and I keep drifting off, but I keep coming back here to this room and these people. One day, I don't remember which day, John, my father, takes my hand and says, *Lara, you were in a horrible car crash. Your best friend Lily died. You didn't but you've been in a coma for a very long time. Do you understand that?*

And I fall asleep again but there are no dreams; no other places. I keep waking up to the bright room with all the happy faces of my family so happy to have me back and nurse Joan and Dr. Jacobson and finally I allow myself to relax into this which I don't remember either but seems to be filled with people who care about me and maybe that's enough.

Maybe just all of them wanting the best for me is all you get no matter that you remember nothing. My mother, Mary, is stroking my arm and humming. I close my eyes but after a few moments, I recognize what she's humming. And I've heard it before. In an elevator. And the sanest part of me knows that none of this is real. None of it has been real and I fall asleep with my mother stroking my arm and humming '*I shot a man in Reno just to watch him die*'.

* * *

Lara wakes to someone nudging her shoulder. She's in her cell on the Fourth Flour but it's dark and everyone is gone. Not quite everyone.

Sarah is nudging her urgently.

"What?" Lara says, her throat tight and sore.

"None of this has been real," Sarah says. "You know that right?"

Lara nods. "Yes. But is this? Now?"

"Yes. And you need to leave it."

"But what was all of it?" Lara asks, so tired so she can barely open her eyes.

Sarah kneels next to the thin bed. "So many timelines and visions of what could have been or may have been or has been and you survived them all. You didn't make the wrong choices. And when you had to, you made the right choices."

"It doesn't have to be this way," Lara whispered, more to herself than Sarah.

"No. It doesn't."

Lara clutches Sarah's arm. "I didn't kill them."

"Of course you didn't," Sarah says. "Seth killed them in one timeline and he killed you too. In this one, Legion, the man you think of as Joey, killed them."

"Are they alive somewhere?" Lara asks. "Somewhere? Some time?"

Sarah shakes her head. "No. They never really existed. They were a memory given to you, to make you think you were real."

"I'm not real?" Lara finds that the easiest thing to believe.

"You are," Sarah says. "But you were made. The Shadow made you. And your brother. Hoping that together, you'd be the key."

"Key to what?" Lara whispers. "Brother? I don't understand."

"You saw some realities and many possibilities. It is your gift and your curse. You're special, Lara. That's why they want you. That's why we wanted you. But I know that's wrong. You have to go where what's special about you can make a difference. To do what you believe is best. You're different. And different is needed."

"For what? What are you talking about?"

"The Shadow made you," Sarah said. "But you escaped and came here. They made one of their own out of you trying to understand what they cannot understand and he's coming here for you. You have to leave before he gets here. And he's close. You have to escape."

Sarah lies down on the hospital bed and curls into Lara's body. Lara turns as much as she's able, to spoon as close as she can to Sarah and asks, "What will happen now? How can I escape?"

Gunfire echoes in the building.

"We're on the Fourth Floor," Sarah says. "You've got to go to the Fifth. The Fifth Floor."

"There isn't one," Sarah says. "This is the top floor."

Sarah runs a hand over Lara's forehead, soothing, calming. "There is. In here. In your mind. It's awareness. The Fifth Awareness."

* * *

Doctor Jenkins cowers behind one of the security contractors as he fires controlled bursts down the hallway. She looks over her shoulder, at the white phone at the end of the hallway, internally debating what to do.

The brief glance she'd had of the intruders indicated the two men only had knives and a woman with a bow and arrow of all things. What could two men with knives and that woman do against these highly armed guards? But how had they even gotten up here? This floor was completely secure.

"Cover me," she says, and then starts to run down the hall.

A burst of fire behind her, then a strange gurgling noise. Halfway down the hall, she risks a glance over her shoulder. An arrow has pierced the guard's throat, the point coming out the back, the spine severed. He falls to the floor, that heavy, instantly dead fall, lacking all grace.

The two men, one in black, the other in a gray coverall, each armed with a knife, were flanking the woman who had a short bow in her hand.

* * *

"It's time to go." Sarah lets go of Lara and gets off the bed.

Lara sits up, her head throbbing in pain, her arms pinned in by the straitjacket. "But go where? How?"

"That only you can do," Sarah says, not helpful at all.

* * *

The phone is still ringing. Doctor Jenkins reaches for it, but staggers forward by the arrow punching into her back and coming out her chest. She stares at it in disbelief.

She's still looking at it when Legion grabs her hair, pulls her head back, and slits her throat, then tosses her aside. Lukas yanks Jenkins's key card off the lanyard

Martha stops at the door to a room and gestures.

Lukas waves the card and the locks clicks.

Legion shoves the door open and all three enter.

* * *

Lara looks at the woman and two men. "Martha."

Sarah faces the intruders. "You cannot have her."

Martha lifts her bow, an arrow ready. "You can't either."

"I know," Sarah says. "She belongs to no one."

"I can hear you," Lara complains, struggling with the straitjacket.

"I am *We*!" Lukas cries out. He surprises Martha by grabbing her bow and tearing it out of her hands.

Legion reacts instinctively, jamming the point of his dagger into Lukas's back.

Lukas straightens, turning hard, ripping the hilt of the dagger out of Legion's hand. He staggers forward.

Lara slides out of the bed, her cheap slippers on the concrete floor.

Sarah makes to intercept him, but Lara says, "No."

Lukas puts his hands out and Lara takes them. He looks into her eyes and smiles. "Sister. I see finally. So random but so real. You might be it. The *One* who can change things. It doesn't have to be this way."

"Get out of the way," Martha orders.

115

Lukas turns and Lara sees the dagger sticking out of his back. She holds her hands up and for a moment everyone in the room is still: Martha, arrow notched and aimed; Legion at her side; Sarah standing next to her; and Lukas, dying in front of her.

* * *

I know this is real. As real as everything else, but even more so. I'm at the center of a hurricane that formed somewhere far away and has swept over me. The hurricane makes no sense, but that doesn't matter right now. I can't hold this eye much longer. Something has to give.

The Fifth Floor?

I look up and I begin to see. A golden orb, three feet in diameter, held by two hands, the rest of the arms fading into nothing. The hands are black and blistered as if the orb was on fire, but it just glows now. Pulsing. Almost alive.

I reach up and take it from the hands, relieving them of the burden and they're gone. The orb isn't hot. It is surprisingly light, but it pulses, as if alive. The surface isn't smooth but covered with two-inch strands, all moving in patterns that at first appear random to me.

But like the writing, I begin to understand. They are timelines. Hundreds of them, thousands of them.

It's a map.

"Go." It's Sarah's voice; she's beginning to move. The boy who said he's my brother is falling to the floor in slow motion, a dagger in his back, an arrow in his chest. An arrow he's taken that Martha meant for me. She's drawing another one, very slowly.

The man next to her, it's Joey, is charging toward me, but so slowly.

I look into the orb, losing the here, the now, searching for a safe place, no, not a safe place, a place where I have to go, to make a difference.

My destiny.

I see it. I grab it.

Our Present: Area 51

THE SNAKE WAS BEHIND the two men waiting, a jet-engine tilt-rotor plane that, according to the Department of Defense, was still being computer simulated and not yet in production. Eagle, the pilot, had been flying one for four years for the Nightstalkers, and now, as a member of the Time Patrol, had access to it when needed.

"Who are the new Nightstalkers?" Eagle asked. It was a question that had been on the edge of his brain ever since being "recruited" into the Time Patrol.

"Bunch of yahoos," Colonel Orlando said. "Never be the same as you guys. Plus, without Rifts to shut, they spend most of their time cranking their yank. Or is it yanking their crank? Working routine stuff like stolen biological agents, nuke stuff, lab mishaps, containment failures. The usual dumb scientist stuff. Be glad you moved on. The scientists seem to be getting dumber." From the tone of his voice, it was clear he was not happy that Eagle and the others had moved on.

"The Ranch the same?" Eagle asked.

"Yeah," Orlando said. "The new Nightstalkers headquarter out of Area 51 for now. It's just as you guys left it."

"Good," Eagle said.

The plane that had just touched down in front of them decelerated. It was a twin-engine jet with a single blue stripe down the side. No tail number, no other markings. It didn't exist to the FAA. It didn't have a transponder. There were lumps under the wings that an observant man could tell housed anti-missile defenses and some offensive capability. Both Eagle and Orlando were observant men.

The plane halted fifty feet away. The front left door opened out and down, providing a short staircase. There was no one for almost ten seconds.

"Geez," Orlando complained. "You remember the Army, Eagle. Any time you get a tasking for warm bodies, you never send your best people. You send the folks you wanna get rid of."

Then a big man dressed in nondescript khakis was framed in the exit. He paused and peered about, saw Orlando and Eagle, then looked past

117

them to the Snake. He looked over his shoulder and said something, then came down the steps with the swagger of, well, a big man; used to dominating whatever setting he was in.

He was followed by a woman, dressed the same. She was young, blond, blue-eyed, and beautiful in that not-quite-a-real-person, thin, tall, model sort of way. She also came down the stairs with the aura of one used to being watched at all times, for reasons different than that of the man.

"I think they sent her to the wrong place," Orlando muttered.

"Don't judge a book by the cover," Eagle said.

"I don't read books."

A Russian soldier came next, his hand on the shoulder of a young woman confined in a straitjacket. Her head was close-shaven, just a dark stubble. She was of average height, skinny to the point of anorexia, and seemed resigned to her fate.

"That's just great," Orlando said.

The big man walked up to Orlando and Eagle, not bothering to wait for the others. "I am—" he began in a Russian accent.

"You're nobody," Orlando cut him off. "No names. We do the naming. For now, you're Boris." The blonde woman arrived, having heard the exchange. Before she could speak, Orlando also christened her. "And you're Princess. And you're"—He looked at the girl in the straightjacket with the scars all over her head—"Lara. Welcome to Area 51."

* * *

EAGLE GLANCED ACROSS the cockpit of the Snake at Orlando. "Are you sure?"

Orlando shrugged. "What's the worst that can happen?"

"Someone dies."

"People die every day."

"We could *all* die," Eagle said.

"That's the whole point of the test." Orlando pulled an oversized flask out of his pocket, unscrewed the lid, took a deep drink, and then offered it to Eagle.

"I'm flying," Eagle said. He had the Snake at 10,000 feet altitude, having taken off as soon as the three boarded. Orlando had unbuckled the arms of the young woman's straitjacket, and then directed all three to go up the ramp into the cargo bay. Eagle had then flown the Snake, almost vertical, gaining altitude and circling, but not moving away from the position over the airfield.

"In the old days," Orlando said, "pilots had balls. Big brass ones. A little drink wouldn't have scared them. Hell, they were supposed to drink."

"My shoulder is killing me," Eagle said. "I should be on painkillers, but I'm not. You think I'm going to take a drink if I can't take something for the pain?"

"You *could* take something for the pain," Orlando pointed out, waggling the flask. "You *choose* not to."

Eagle shook his head.

"It's always about choice," Orlando said. "Remember that. And hell, this thing can fly itself on autopilot." He stood up from the co-pilot's seat, which reminded Eagle he'd never buckled in on takeoff or put on his parachute as per SOP.

Eagle sighed and flipped on the autopilot.

Orlando stood in the passageway between the cockpit and the cargo hold. "Yo!" he yelled to be heard over the sound of the two jet engines. "Listen up."

Boris, Princess, and Lara were on the red web jump seats along the outer edge of the bay. Boris and Princess sat on the same side, but with enough distance between them to indicate they wanted nothing to do with each other. Lara sat on the other, cross-legged, eyes closed. She didn't open them at Orlando's shout. The harness was still around her body even though her hands were free. She seemed used to it.

"Why are we here?" Boris shouted back.

"They didn't tell you?" Orlando said. "Oh, that's right. They weren't supposed to tell you. You've all volunteered to try out for the most super-secret, best of the best, covert unit in the world."

"I did not volunteer," Princess complained.

"Who does?" Orlando said. "If you really were volunteers, we wouldn't want you. It would mean you're stupid. We don't do stupid here."

"Where is here?" Boris demanded. "What is this Area 51?"

"Now, thirty years ago," Orlando said, "that question might be sorta legit. But seriously, son. You don't follow the news? You didn't see *Independence Day*? The original or the sequel? I hate sequels, although *Aliens* was pretty good. And the second Godfather. That was good too. Maybe better, but it's debatable." Orlando pointed. "That way is the Nevada Test Site. Seven-hundred and thirty-nine—"

"Seven-hundred and forty," Eagle corrected him.

"Seven-hundred and forty nuclear weapons have gone off there," Orlando said. "Pretty good barrier. Area 51 is just about below us. Groom Lake. Big runway. Air Force and NASA test their high-speed stuff out here since it's pretty far from anywhere. Vegas is that way," Orlando pointed in a different direction, and Eagle didn't have the heart to tell him he was off. It really didn't matter. "I have a theory," Orlando said. "People go to L.A., to suffer, and Vegas to die."

Boris and Princess exchanged confused glances. Lara still hadn't opened her eyes or indicate she heard any of this.

"Y'all want to go to Vegas?" Orlando asked. "Or do you want to go to L.A.?"

Boris stood up. "I do not like this."

"I was just joking," Orlando said. "You're not going to either place." He looked at Boris. "And no one gives a rat's ass what you like or don't like." He reached up and hit a button.

The noise level in the cargo bay increased dramatically as a crack appeared in the back. The ramp lowered, while the top portion went up into the tail section. Both moved until the ramp was level and locked in place.

Boris looked at that, then back at Eagle and Orlando. "What is this?" he yelled.

Princess edged away from the ramp toward the cockpit. One of her hands was tight to her side.

"She's got a knife," Eagle yelled into Orlando's ear, the equivalent of a whisper.

"I know," Orlando said. "Saw her take it off Lara's guard. Idiot didn't even know she lifted it."

Orlando pulled a grenade out of his pocket then held it up so they could all see it. "Choices!" he yelled, and then he pulled the pin, knelt, and rolled it to the center of the cargo bay.

Everyone was frozen for a moment.

* * *

Everyone is still as I see it all playing out, the possibilities. The grenade exploding here, inside the plane, all of us dying, except they wouldn't do that, these two soldiers, they love life too much, which is strange for men in their occupation.

So, it won't explode here.

There's another point to this. A test. I'm so tired of tests.

Princess will run, as if there is anywhere to run to.

Boris won't do anything. He's mean, a bully, used to intimidating, but will fold when pushed. Claude would have cut him down to size in a moment.

Strange, I almost miss Claude.

The black man with the scars, he's interesting. I can literally feel his brain working, so much in there. So much information. Amazing.

He's interesting enough for me to want to pass his test.

* * *

Princess ran for the cockpit, away from the grenade. Boris was frozen, eyes wide, staring at it, less than five feet in front of him.

Lara darted forward, scooped it up, then continued her run and swan-dived off the back ramp, grenade in hand.

"That was different," Orlando said, reaching for his flask.

"Jerk," Eagle yelled at Orlando as he ran to the ramp and dove out.

He spread his legs and arms akimbo, getting stable and oriented. He saw Lara tumbling in the air. He pulled his arms into his sides, clamped his legs together, and dove, angled straight down.

Using just his hands, like fins for direction, he accelerated toward her.

Eagle began making up the distance between the two of them, losing altitude the entire way.

Six thousand feet, the altimeter warned via his earpiece.

He saw her arm move, tossing the grenade away.

Five thousand feet.

Eagle was stunned when the grenade exploded, a brief flash, the sound lost in the air rushing by.

"Double Jerk, Orlando!" Eagle screamed as he adjusted his track slightly.

Four thousand feet. She was fifty feet below.

Eagle blinked as he realized she was slowing her spin. She was experimenting, thrusting an arm this way, tucking a leg that way. Why, when she had no chute?

* * *

This won't be so bad. Splat.

They say you're dead before the nervous system can transmit the pain to the brain.

I briefly wonder who they are that says that. I wonder where I read that little tidbit?

I lift my arms over my head, enjoying the air ripping by as I fall.

Beats weeding.

I see the black man and he's so graceful. He's using just his cupped hands, the arc of his foot, to maneuver.

Impressive.

121

He's trying to save me.
I'm overwhelmed.
He doesn't even know me.

* * *

Three thousand feet the altimeter warned Eagle.

Ten feet away.

She was looking at him, no longer tumbling. She'd assumed an odd position. Legs together, arms spread wide above her head. Feet straight down toward the rapidly approaching desert.

She looks like an angel, Eagle thought, apropos of nothing of importance at the moment because they were both going to pile driver in.

Eagle over-adjusted then bumped into her, chest-to-chest.

She smiled at him.

One thousand feet.

Eagle only had time to clip a single snap link from his lowering line into her straitjacket harness, and then he jerked the ripcord.

His parachute blossomed.

Eagle was jerked upright, and then he felt the abrupt tightening of his harness as she hit the end of the fifteen-foot lowering line. He barely had time to look down before she struck the ground, then he was down, hitting hard, feet on either side of her body. He collapsed to his knees, straddling her.

"Frak me," Eagle muttered. He glanced down at the young woman lying between his legs. Now that he was this close, he noticed the poorly healed scars underneath the hair struggling to grow back on her scalp. A jigsaw puzzle of them.

Lara was still smiling. "He is a crazy man."

"He is," Eagle agreed. She had an American accent, not Russian. Who exactly was she?

"I like him."

"I don't."

* * *

I'm in the back of a truck. Two men on either side of me. I can't quite tell if they're guards keeping me here or to protect me.

I don't care because I can hear them, the two men from the plane, talking about me, even though they're driving away. It's weird. But fun.

"A live grenade?" *The black man is upset with the older man.*

"It wouldn't have been a real test if it weren't a real grenade."

"I should—"

"Oh, relax. It had altimeter arming built in. Wouldn't have gone off above eight thousand feet. If none of those yahoos had done anything, it would have just rolled around, and we could have kicked it out or put the pin back in. But she did something. Damned impressive."

I feel like I've just had brought in the heaviest bucket. I wonder if they give cookies?

"But why have it explode on the way down?"

"She didn't, and doesn't, know there was an altimeter arming device. She's always going to believe it was live from the get-go."

Not really, I think.

"What if one of the others had done that?" *the black man asks.* "I was able to hook into her straitjacket with the lowering line. But if one of the other—"

"They didn't. I been doing this for a long time. I didn't actually expect anyone to jump *out* with it. Jump on it. Try to throw it out. Run away. No one has ever grabbed it and jumped with it. What's as interesting as Lara jumping is you going after her."

"So she's suicidal," *the black man says and I sense my cookie disappearing.*

"You said she tossed the grenade away after she left the plane."

"Yeah, but she didn't have a chute."

"If she were suicidal, she'd have held on to the grenade."

I'd known the grenade was real. But not about the altimeter. So, what I can see is limited. I need to remember that.

"But, again, she didn't have a chute."

"Maybe she knew you'd come after her?"

"How could she know that?"

That makes me think. Did I know the man named Eagle would come after me?

"Good question."

"Any problems with the autopilot landing?"

"Nah. Machines can do stuff like that, but they can't think. They don't got the instincts a real pilot has."

"Boris?"

"Pissed in his pants. Seriously, if that's the best the Russkies got, I don't know why we worry about them. He's on a plane home. In the old days, they'd greet him with a bullet to the back of the head for getting sent back. Now, they'll probably kiss him."

"Princess?" *Eagle asks.*

"Had to shoot her. Not fatal, but she's gonna need a knee replacement. She tried to cut me. Women. Can't trust 'em.'"

That reminds me of Doctor Jacobson. He hated women. Had hated. I knew whatever timeline that was, that he was no longer part of it.

"Ms. Jones was a woman," *the old man says.*

"She was Ms. Jones."

"Moms is a woman."

"She's Moms."

I wonder who these people are. They both speak of the women with respect I can sense even as their presence grows fainter.

"Scout?" *Eagle asks.*

"I like her. Something about the kid."

There's another kid here? Part of this, whatever this is? Best of the best?

"Why'd you call her Lara?" *the old man asks Eagle. I worry, because I'd edged him automatically, not wanting to be Lily or anyone else. Not any more.*

"First thing that came to mind when I saw her."

"Doctor Zhivago?" *Eagle asks and I hear music, beautiful music.*

"Who?"

"She's not Russian," *Eagle says.* "Sounds American. How'd she end up with the Russians?"

"How'd she end up in a straitjacket?"

"Where are they taking her?"

"Your boss, Dane, wants to talk to her."

And then I can't hear them any more. But I can still hear the music. So pretty. I suppose I'll meet this Dane soon.

I hope he's not like Doctor Jacobson. But I think these people are different.

We'll see.

The Possibility Palace: Down the Hall

DANE SAT ACROSS FROM LARA, regarding her without comment. Frasier was on his side of the table, leafing through a thin file, translated from Russian.

"What little is in here, is heavily redacted," Frasier complained. "But from what I can read, she did some very, very bad things."

"Bad things," Lara whispered. "Yes. Bad things." She was speaking to herself as if she were alone in the room.

"We've all done bad things," Dane said.

Frasier shoved the folder over to him. "Not like this."

Dane didn't have to read it. "I know."

Frasier pointed out the obvious. "And she's not Russian. How did she end up over there?"

"Here, there," Lara said. "Now, then. What does it matter?"

"I'm sure it's an interesting story," Dane said.

"The Fifth Floor," Lara said.

"What's that?" Frasier asked.

Dane shook his head. "Not now. We'll get to that." His focus was on the girl. "You're going to make a choice."

Lara nodded. "Whether to join the Time Patrol."

"How do you know that?" Dane asked.

She'd been brought here unconscious, through the Gate from underneath the Met. The only part of the Possibility Palace she'd seen so far was this room.

"It is all everyone here thinks about," Lara said.

"You know what people are thinking?" Frasier asked.

"At times." She smiled. "Why do you think they sent me in the straitjacket?"

"What am I thinking right now?" Dane asked.

"I don't do parlor tricks," Lara said. She shrugged. "I don't know. It doesn't work like that. But if enough people think or feel something, it is easy to"—She paused, searching for the word—"see."

"The Sight," Dane said. He tapped a finger on the tabletop. "In the course of history, there are billions and billions of lives. The reality is, few of those individual lives make an impact. That's not to say that in their personal lives, for their family, their friends, and even their enemies, all those people aren't important. But if any of those people ceased to exist, blinked out of existence, the course of history would not change."

Lara stared at him, expressionless.

"Even those we think are historically significant," Dane continued, "whether by the weight of their entire life, or by a single, momentous action, such as Oswald assassinating Kennedy, might not even be important, since someone else might do the same."

"We're replaceable," Lara said.

"Pretty much everyone," Dane said.

"Who am I replacing?" she asked. "There's a group of sad people here. They miss someone."

"That's not important right now," Dane said.

"Would they miss me some day?" Lara murmured. "It would be nice to be missed. I doubt they miss me on the Fourth Floor. But maybe they do, but not for good reasons."

As Frasier opened his mouth to say something, Dane gave a subtle signal with his hand, silencing him. "What is needed to be a member of the Time Patrol, Lara, is that you are a person who will never, ever, use our capability and go back and change something for personal reasons. Every person has something in their past, some point where we wish we had chosen differently. Many points, probably. But you can't ever use time travel for personal reasons."

He held up three fingers. "You now have to make a decision to take one of three paths. First, you may choose not to choose. To walk away. Second, you may go back to that key moment and change what happened. Third—"

"You will not allow that second choice if it changes history," Lara said.

"True," Dane said. "But as I said, most of us aren't that important. If you choose to go back, and it doesn't affect the timeline—and it most likely won't—you *will* be allowed to go back but that will be it and you will never be Time Patrol. And if you begin to interfere in the point you go back to by knowing the future, you will receive a visit from one of our operatives at that time, and be Sanctioned."

"Killed."

"Yes."

"I imagine that will also be the result if I choose not to choose."

"No," Dane said. "You'll be sent home."

"'Home'?" Lara laughed. "What home? The Fourth Floor? Before that? Which home? Which person?" Lara shook her head. "You will not allow me to leave this place, knowing what I know."

"You won't know what you know," Frasier said. "We'll wipe your memory from the time you arrived at Area 51 until just before you get back."

"Ah," Lara said. "But how do you know this key moment?"

"We know," Dane said. "We have our own people with the Sight."

"And my final option...?" Lara asked.

"Accept who you are now," Dane said. "Where you are now. All that has happened to shape you into who you are. And choose to be part of the Time Patrol."

"When do I have to make this choice?" she asked.

"Now," Dane replied.

"I can really go back and change it?"

"Yes." Dane said. "We both know the moment."

"Do you?" Lara asked, realizing he knew the moment, but not the timeline.

A flicker of uncertainty crossed Dane's face.

"And if I change it," Lara said, "that won't change the timeline?"

"No."

* * *

They think I have a choice. They think me memories of my family are real. That there is a time I can go back to and save them. A family that never existed. They don't know I was made by the Shadow.

They know so much, but there's so much they don't know.

I feel tears, sadness for their ignorance.

I look down, knowing I have to pretend, learned that on the Fourth Floor. I wait an appropriate amount of time, and then look up at Dane.

"I will stay here and be Time Patrol."

I feel Dane's satisfaction with my decision. He has another recruit. This Dane, he has some of it. He can see more than most. Touch the Fourth Awareness.

But he has no clue about the Fifth.

They, this Time Patrol, are holding on to the past, keeping it intact, in order to hold on to their present.

It doesn't have to be this way.

They want me to help them keep things as they are.
I don't think so.

THE END
For Now

The Time Patrol

There once was a place called Atlantis. Ten thousand years ago, it was attacked by a force known only as the Shadow, on the same day over the course of six years. The last attack led to Atlantis being obliterated to the point where it is just a legend.

There are many Earth timelines. The Shadow comes from one of those alternate timelines (or perhaps more than one). It is attacking our timeline by punching bubbles into our past that can last no more than twenty-four hours. In each bubble, the Shadow is trying to change our history and cause a time ripple.

By itself, a single time ripple can be dealt with, corrected, and absorbed. But a significant time ripple that is unchecked can become a Cascade. Six Cascades can combine to become a Time Tsunami.

That would be the end of our timeline and our existence.

To achieve its goal, the Shadow attacks six points in time simultaneously, the same date in different years.

The Time Patrol's job is to keep our timeline intact.

The Time Patrol sends an agent back to each of those six dates to keep history the same.

About Bob Mayer

Bob Mayer is the grandfather of two future leaders of the Resistance Against the Machines, a NY Times Bestselling author, graduate of West Point, former Green Beret (including commanding an A-Team). He's had over 80 books published including the #1 series Area 51, Atlantis, Time Patrol and The Green Berets. Born in the Bronx, having traveled the world (usually not tourist spots), he now lives peacefully with his wife, and dogs in an undisclosed location.

For free eBooks and more information:
http://bobmayer.com

www.ingramcontent.com/pod-product-compliance
Lightning Source LLC
Chambersburg PA
CBHW030537130626
46552CB00006B/2306